Bringing Home the Cost of War

J. Thomas Hennessey, Jr. PhD

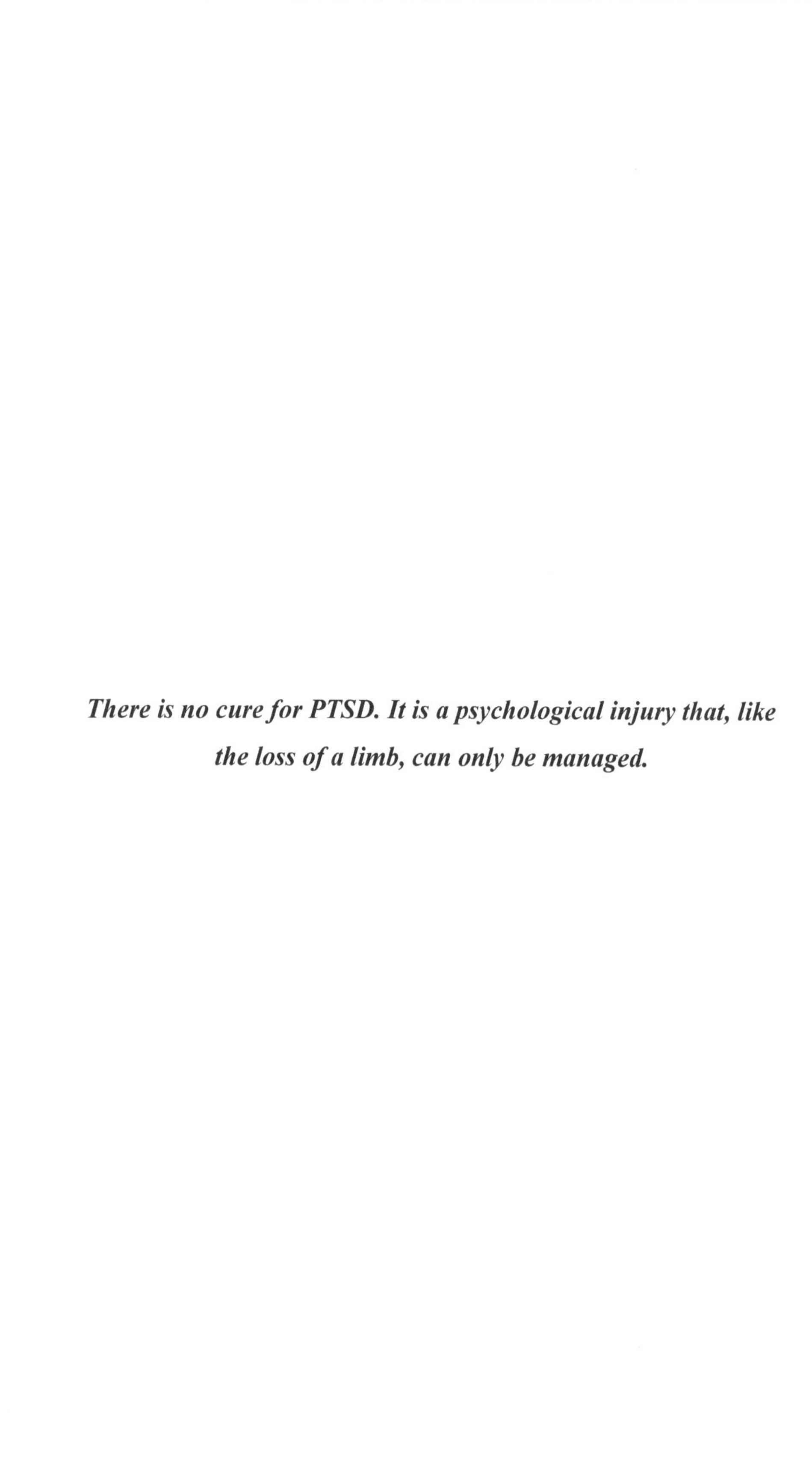

There is no cure for PTSD. It is a psychological injury that, like the loss of a limb, can only be managed.

Table of Contents

Disclaimer:

This is a fictional account of one officer's struggle with PTSD and how he learned to manage it. The names and places are fictional, while the events actually happened.

Prologue

This book is dedicated to the veterans of the Vietnam War. We didn't appreciate what Post Traumatic Stress Disorder (PTSD) was back then, and I suspect our understanding of it is better now. I offer no solutions, no easy "fix-me-ups." All I can do is tell a story about one young man's struggles and how he found a way forward. It is not the story of just one soldier but of many who experienced PTSD and helped others overcome the challenges faced by each of them.

After the Battle of Ia Drang in 1965, during the Vietnam War, the United States Armed Forces established casualty-notification teams and began making death notifications in person. Before this change, the military relied on telegrams, often delivered by taxi cab drivers, to inform families of the death of a service member. This method was criticized as impersonal and lacking compassion. The push for this change was influenced by the efforts of Julia Compton Moore, the late Lt. Gen. Hal Moore's wife, who attended funerals for those who fell while under her husband's command and advocated for a more respectful approach. Her actions led to the Army creating casualty notification teams consisting of a uniformed officer and a noncommissioned officer, or a chaplain when available.

I am afraid this story is going to be too familiar for the hundred thousand-plus veterans who saw heavy combat in Vietnam. For those millions who supported us, the combat troops, thank you for all you did. Without the beans and the bullets you provided so well, many of us would not be here now. For all veterans, I hope you find this tale one that encourages you to seek help when needed and to provide support to other veterans wherever it can be helpful. This is a journey of acknowledgment that illustrates one cannot succeed alone. With those less-than-happy words, I begin.

Chapter One: How the Story Begins

If I've read it once, I've felt the same emotions all veterans have shared countless times: that first deep breath upon arriving in Vietnam is something that stays with you, even if it's hard to put into words. The overwhelming blend of fish sauce, charcoal smoke, and human waste, carried on a sweltering 95-degree, 95% humidity breeze, is a sensation that jolts the senses. We all remember it as our first "taste" of Vietnam. Those first two days flew by in a whirlwind of orientations and lectures, filled with instructions on what to do and what to avoid, as well as an understanding of who we were fighting and why. When my unit assignment was posted, I was directed back to the airfield for a flight to Pleiku. The next day, I found myself in the field, stepping into the role of a leader for a platoon I would serve for the next twelve months. It's a journey that many of us hold close to our hearts, filled with both challenges and moments of connection.

During that first tour in Vietnam, I was a dedicated learner. As a new Lieutenant, I was trying to soak up as much experience as I could. Often feeling inadequate for the job, my saving grace was the outstanding noncommissioned officers I was fortunate to work with. One of the more memorable events occurred when I had been in country for two months, leading my platoon, in combat in the central highlands. It was during one of our heaviest engagements that an enemy mortar round slightly wounded me. After the fight, we policed the battlefield, treated the other wounded, and prepared to continue the mission. The platoon medic filled out the casualty tag all wounded receive, tied it to my web gear, and said,

"There's room on the last chopper, Lieutenant."

As I insisted that I didn't need to be medically evacuated, my platoon sergeant, a no-nonsense veteran, pulled me aside,

"Lieutenant, you did well. Get patched up and come on back. The troops need you."

That's the affirmation a young Lieutenant needs to keep going. I swallowed my pride and got on the chopper. I walked from the helipad to the entrance to the hospital and was immediately asked to leave my weapons with an armorer, who gave me a receipt for my M16 rifle and .45 pistol. The next few days, after doctors picked pieces of metal out of me, I enjoyed hot showers and hot food, things I had not had in more than a month. I had been sewn up quickly, injected with a large amount of antibiotics, and given meds for the parasites that had taken residence in my body. I visited with the two other members of the platoon who were evacuated with me. One was going to be sent to the States, the other to Japan. I doubt either one would be returning to the platoon. My release was contingent upon keeping my surgical incisions covered and promising to take the prescribed antibiotics.

When I returned to the platoon after a week, I felt like I finally had some idea of what I was doing. The central highlands were physically demanding, and the North Vietnamese Army was infiltrating South Vietnam through those mountains. I likely lost another ten pounds over the next couple of months. We experienced multiple firefights, and I lost another half dozen soldiers during the following ten months, most of them wounded and evacuated to hospitals in the rear.

If navigating the hills and mountains wasn't challenging enough, malaria was rampant in our area of the highlands. I can still taste the bitter Dapsone pill we took every day for the peculiar type of malaria prevalent in the central highlands. I learned many years later that Dapsone is a treatment for leprosy. Some researchers discovered that leper colonies located in areas with falciparum malaria had a remarkably low incidence of malaria among the lepers. So, I suppose what is good enough for lepers is good enough for soldiers.

It's still sometimes hard to remember that we often didn't know what day of the week it was. Our days were marked by the passage of dawn, midday, evening, and night. Each had a different set of requirements, a different set of dangers, and either incessant cold rain during the monsoon season or oppressive heat in the summer. Only those who have survived in the central highlands can confirm that the winter nights in the higher elevations can be cold, particularly when it rains. The alternating cold and heat played havoc on our bodies, and the relentless day-to-day movement through the highlands caused more than one soldier to stop taking his Dapsone, so that he would get malaria and be evacuated.

Within six months, half the platoon had rotated back to the States, and a half dozen troops were medically evacuated after being wounded. Most were returned to the States. The four soldiers killed during those six months were a loss we all felt. One in particular was a favorite because he looked about 14 and acted that way. I remember the faces of many of my soldiers, but that fresh face with its mischievous smile is one I cannot forget.

As my twelve-month tour of duty came to a close, I bid farewell to the soldiers I had led and loved like brothers. I thanked the newest platoon sergeant for his work and encouraged him to mentor the new platoon leader as he and his predecessor had mentored me. My departure from the same airfield where I had arrived twelve months prior was surreal. Replacements, all in new jungle fatigues, looked at those of us about to leave with mixed emotions. Some were openly curious, while others studiously avoided looking at us. As the airliner took off, many soldiers let out shouts of joy. As I looked around the cabin, I could identify the soldiers who had, like me, just come in from combat in the bush. They were quiet and contemplative about their survival. On the other hand, the soldiers who had spent their year in the rear and probably never heard a shot fired in anger were loud and boisterous in their joy of leaving Vietnam. On that Freedom Bird flight back to the States, I remembered those we lost and hoped their sacrifice would be remembered by more than just those with whom they served.

I spent two weeks with my family in Florida and then headed to Fort Benning, Georgia, for the Infantry Officers' Advanced Course. I was promoted to Captain while I was on leave and picked up my new "railroad tracks" when I arrived. This second time at Ft Benning was the most important in my life because I met Alene Harris within weeks of my arrival. The ten-month Infantry Officer Advanced Course is intended to prepare newly promoted Captains to command companies and perform staff duties at the battalion level. Compared to being an infantry platoon leader in Vietnam, the months at Benning were a piece of cake. One evening, shortly after the course began, I met Alene at a Happy Hour in the Officers Club, where she and some of her friends were having drinks. Her looks and poise struck me, and I immediately asked her out on a date.

Alene and I had multiple dates over the next two months. It was clear, at least to me, after the first couple of dates, that this was the woman I wanted to spend my life with. Before I made my proposal, I knew I would be returning to Vietnam, and I was upfront with her about that. As an Army brat and the daughter of a retired Sergeant Major, she knew as much about deployments and long absences as anyone. I made a reservation at one of the better restaurants in Columbus, and over candlelight and wine, I proposed. I was overjoyed that she felt the same and agreed to marry me. She asked why I hadn't proposed earlier, because she knew after the first few dates that she and I had a connection that would result in marriage. I suppose I'm just a slow learner.

We set the wedding for three months before I graduated. She said she would stay with her folks in Columbus until I returned. Since we were not permitted to take leave during the course, our honeymoon was a three-day weekend in Myrtle Beach. My folks in Florida were disappointed that they couldn't be at the wedding. I assured them we would visit the first chance we had. Alene's parents were great and even offered to have us stay with them until I left for Vietnam. I was more than glad to accept their hospitality because BOQ (bachelor officers' quarters) never looked so forlorn after we returned from Myrtle Beach. The months we had before I left were spent getting to know Alene's extended family, finishing my coursework, and even spending some time with the Infantry Officer's Basic Course. Many of us were asked to become mentors for the newly commissioned infantry officers.

The purpose of the program was to have combat-experienced officers mentor new Lieutenants who would almost certainly be in Vietnam within the year. One of my more interesting experiences with a new lieutenant I was mentoring was a young Lieutenant who struggled to pass the written exams. He did well on every graded event outside the classroom, whether it was leadership, land navigation, or tactical maneuvers. When I asked him why he had so much trouble, after all, he was a college graduate. This young man, standing at six feet five inches and probably weighing 250 pounds, confessed that he couldn't read well. When I asked what he did in college, his response was surprising.

"Captain, I was recruited to play football at Georgia, not to go to class. I was told that I would be able to play pro ball and not worry about anything in school.

"Well, Lieutenant, why are you here?"

"Sir, I was drafted by the Atlanta Falcons in the first two years they were in the NFL. I played nose guard and, honest to God, I got my ass beat every Sunday those two years. We never won a game. I figured Vietnam couldn't be much worse, so I volunteered to go on active duty."

Trying hard to contain my amusement, I smiled, "Well, Lieutenant, the only thing I can guarantee you about being a platoon leader in Vietnam is that you won't get your ass beat every Sunday. You will get it beat every day. I recommend you learn how to keep your head down because you make a huge target." The short mentoring program didn't do much to help my unease. I was certain more than a few of those I mentored would be coming home in body bags, the very large Lieutenant included.

Returning to Vietnam as a married Captain was far different from going to Vietnam for the first time as a bachelor Lieutenant. About to lead many more soldiers in combat, I felt an added responsibility to apply what I had learned the hard way during my time as a platoon leader. Now, as a "seasoned veteran" at 26, I was supposed to lead more than a hundred soldiers on combat missions. Little did I realize that in 1968, there were only a few noncommissioned officers in my company older than me.

Alene and I said a tough goodbye at the airport. I kissed her salty tears and assured her I would be back in one piece before she knew it.

I could smell her perfume and the soft brush of that beautiful, blond hair on my face as I walked onto the plane. I was determined to keep my promise to her.

My second arrival in Vietnam was very different from my first. I immediately joined the 3rd Brigade of the 82nd Airborne just after it deployed to Hue to relieve the Marines. During the Tet Offensive of 1968, the Marines retook the Citadel and drove out the North Vietnamese Army. I took over command of Bravo Company, 2nd Battalion, 505th Parachute Infantry Regiment when the Brigade Commander dropped me off at the company's location and said,

"It's yours now, Foster. We will be back in a day or two."

No formal change of command. There was no transition with the old company commander. He had already been pulled out and sent to another unit. I cannot think of a more inauspicious introduction to my new responsibilities.

I found the company command post bunker, ducked into the low entry, and saw two soldiers sitting on ammo boxes manning radios. One of them turned to me,

"Hey, Captain, can I help you?"

"I'm your new company commander. Where are the platoon leaders?"

The soldier almost dropped the handset and replied,

Bringing Home the Cost of War

"Welcome aboard, Sir. I'll call the platoon leaders. Do you want them to come here?"

"Yes, I need to introduce myself and find out what the platoons' missions are."

I was fortunate to have four solid platoon leaders and five veteran platoon sergeants, one of whom I assigned as my field First Sergeant. After a week of learning about the area of operations and the members of the company, I felt I, and we were ready. It was not long until my company ran full tilt into the retreating North Vietnamese Army, and we battled them off and on for ten days. We arrived in the fight with 121 paratroopers, and when we were finally relieved, sixty-one of us walked out. The many wounded and the few dead had been evacuated. I had to go to the mortuary unit and positively identify the two platoon leaders who were lost in the first days. The unzipping of the body bags and seeing the now grey faces of the two young men I knew well remained with me for months. Those first three months were some of the heaviest fighting of the Vietnam War, and we were in the thick of it. For two of those months, Bravo Company was attached to a battalion of the 101st Airborne Division. As the "red-headed stepchild," we spent all our time in the bush and had little or no downtime.

It was only after we rejoined our battalion and were given three days of "stand down" that an appropriate memorial ceremony could be held for those we had lost in the last four months. I choked up when recounting how well the company had done and that we would never forget those we had lost while accomplishing our mission. The First Sergeant performed the traditional roll call where the names of those no longer with us were repeated three times before calling the next name. It seemed to me that every third or fourth name was met with silence. Those silences made the event even more somber. The memorial service on a dry, dusty field, surrounded by the paratroopers I led and loved, was a moment so vivid in my memory that it is no wonder I remember it so well.

Alene dutifully wrote to me daily, reminding me how much she looked forward to my letters, but said she often waited more than a week between them. Time to write letters was few and far between, even if we didn't have to put stamps on the envelopes. I once wrote her a letter about how I felt after losing a young soldier whom I had come to know well. After I read it, I realized it wasn't something I should share with Alene. It was too raw, and writing it was a release that Alene didn't deserve.

My change of command nine months later was a bittersweet event. I was heading home, leaving the troops who had come to depend on me. I hoped that my successor would take care of them at least as well as I did. The short flight to the departure airfield was shared with two other officers from the Brigade who were leaving at the same time. Once we were processed out and loaded on the airliner, it was, as Yogi Berra so eloquently stated, déjà vu all over again. As the plane took off, the reactions of the soldiers on board were much the same as those of the soldiers I had traveled with almost two years ago. The combat soldiers were wearily thankful, and many looked as if the weight of the world had been lifted from their shoulders. The rear echelon soldiers were loud and boisterous in their joy.

When I returned from that second tour, Alene said I was a different person. She said I was the same Jim, but I was changed. Physically, I was thinner, no longer the robust twenty-four-year-old she married between tours in Vietnam. She said it was in my eyes. She said she loved how they were warm and open before. But now they seemed to look right through her. Alene's struggle to understand my change was in her eyes. I realized I had changed, but dismissed it as simply a result of my maturity as an officer leading soldiers in combat.

Alene is the product of a military family; her father was a Korean War veteran. I assumed that any change she saw was from my combat experience. I gotta tell you, the nightmares and strange responses to sudden light and noises concerned me more than Alene's reaction. It took me almost the entire two weeks we spent with her family in Georgia to regain what Alene said was a semblance of my former enthusiastic demeanor. She remarked that I was hyper alert and seemed to be carrying some memory I couldn't explain.

Before I left Vietnam, I received orders to report to ROTC duty at my alma mater, Southern Kentucky University. Alene and I were looking forward to the assignment in Leesburg, Kentucky. We hoped it would be a time we could finally spend some extended time together and even start a family.

Bringing Home the Cost of War

Alene was delighted we could spend most of the leave with her parents in Columbus, Georgia. A quick trip to my parents in Florida rounded out the three weeks of leave. The road trip from Georgia to Kentucky was an extension of our honeymoon; I began to relax as we took our time and explored the small towns along the way. Sitting in a small outdoor café with her blond hair brushing my face was as close to paradise as I could imagine. That four-day trip rekindled the romance we had when I first proposed. As we drove into Leesburg, Kentucky, I could tell it hadn't changed much in the four and a half years I was away. Like any small town centered around a university, I hoped it would be a haven of tranquility for us.

Chapter Two: The ROTC Assignment

Alene and I checked into a motel just outside town and, after dinner at one of my favorite restaurants, decided to visit the campus the next day. That first day driving back on campus after almost five years was surreal. It was like stepping into another world. Less than fifty days ago, I was slogging through a steaming jungle with a forty-pound rucksack, leading 120 paratroopers on a mission to find and destroy enemy soldiers. That memory brought back a rush of adrenaline I recognized as something I also experienced just as the first shots rang out in the jungle. That fleeting thought was followed by a hope that the nightmares and the unusual response to loud noises or bright flashes of light would subside once Alene and I were together for more than a few months. Reflectively, I thought, "Everyone who has been in combat reacts the same way." I thought. After all, when I was wounded the first time or even the second time, no doctor ever asked if I had headaches or trouble sleeping.

The bright July morning revealed how some things had changed since I left almost five years ago. The mini-skirted, bra-less young ladies would have never been seen on campus in the early sixties. Talk about a little distraction! "I guess I'll get used to it soon enough," was my first thought as I parked the car and we began the walk across campus.

Although the buildings hadn't changed, they seemed smaller and closer together. As a 27-year-old with two combat tours in Vietnam, so much of the world I once knew so well had changed. Alene was enthralled by the campus and kept remarking how beautiful it was. I suppose that because it was all so familiar, I had lost the sense of wonder that comes from seeing it for the first time. We walked leisurely across campus to the ROTC building, which was also part of the football stadium. As we approached, I turned to Alene,

"The ROTC building hasn't changed; it's the same old drab concrete I remember."

"Jim, that is one ugly building. It doesn't fit the rest of campus!"

"That's probably why the ROTC detachment is there," I jokingly responded. As we headed back to the car, Alene had one final comment.

"You never told me how beautiful the campus is!"

"I guess after four years, I sort of took it for granted," was my lame response.

A quiet, candlelit dinner at the historic Boone Tavern, in the town next to campus, ended one of our best days in a city that has now taken on an entirely new feel. I found myself looking forward to next Monday when I would report to the ROTC detachment in that drab, concrete building. This ROTC assignment would be a change for us. One that I thought I needed.

The next day, we saw the two-bedroom, two-bath house that the ROTC detachment had located and recommended for us to rent. It was perfect. Alene said more than once, "Plenty of room for family and friends and even some little ones." Less than two miles from campus and in a quiet neighborhood with a few faculty members as neighbors, Alene and I knew this was the right place. I arranged to have our household goods from storage delivered before the ink was dry on the rental agreement. That evening, back at the motel, we began the process of figuring out how to furnish our first home together. Alene had done all the hard work, measuring the rooms and detailing exactly what we needed, from beds to bathroom accessories. I am constantly amazed that this wonderful woman is my wife.

On Monday, I was a bag of mixed feelings as I walked into the familiar ROTC detachment offices. On one hand, I was excited to be here. On the other hand, I had little experience teaching and wondered how I would do. My new green uniform, complete with all the recent ribbons on my left chest, gave me a sense of confidence I hadn't felt before. I was greeted by the Detachment's administrative assistant with a "Welcome aboard, Captain Foster. Please have a seat, we knew you were signing in this morning. The Colonel will see you shortly."

As I looked around the room, it was hard to believe that it had been nearly five years since I repeated the oath of office when commissioned as a Second Lieutenant right here. The Professor of Military Science (PMS) at that time seemed like a younger version of Methuselah—a World War II veteran in his final year of active duty before retirement. Aside from the commissioning ceremony, I can't recall any other interaction I had with the old PMS. When I stepped into the current PMS office, I was pleasantly surprised to see that the

Colonel now commanding the detachment was considerably younger than his predecessor. As I approached Colonel Hewitt, I could tell he was examining me carefully.

After shaking hands with me and offering me a chair, Colonel James Hewitt looked approvingly at me. His first words took me by surprise,

"Jim, you have had twenty-four months in combat, and, from your decorations, you did well. I am happy that the big Army is finally sending some outstanding young officers to ROTC. From my standpoint, things are looking up."

Before I could respond, Hewitt continued,

"I am also glad to see that we are getting some ROTC alumni for the program. You have a lot to share with the cadets. You may remember that we have one of the largest ROTC programs, and each instructor has multiple classes each day. As a history major here at Southern, I assume you will have no problem getting up to speed on the military history classes you will teach Freshmen. Classes begin in mid-August, so you and your wife will have plenty of time to get settled. The staff admin has your office assignment and information on some University-required introductory classes you must take before teaching this Fall. Do you have any questions or concerns?"

"Wow," I thought. "This guy gets right to the point. No question about what I will do for the next few days and weeks."

Bringing Home the Cost of War

My quick response to Colonel Hewitt was "No, sir. I am sure Alene and I will be happy in the house your folks found for us, and I look forward to preparing to teach in the next month."

"Glad you are joining us, Jim. I look forward to hearing more about your time with the 82nd Airborne, the Division I spent most of my time with troops."

The rest of the morning was spent with the administrative staff setting up my office, getting keys to the ROTC offices, and being introduced to some of the other ROTC instructors. I had forgotten that the officers and noncommissioned officers were at summer training camp for ROTC cadets. This annual training requirement for cadets entering their senior year was conducted by ROTC cadre from multiple schools, and cadets came from campuses across the East Coast. Our cadre would return to campus two weeks before the start of the Fall semester.

My office mate, Bob Schindler, was an Air Defense Artillery Officer and also a ROTC commissioned officer from Ohio State. He gave me a warm welcome to the "cave," as the cadre called our offices, because we had no windows. I was glad we had a chance to talk before I finished putting my books and binders away in the bookcase. I opened the conversation,

"Bob, how do you like Leesburg and Southern?"

"It's a great place to live and raise a family. Barbara and I had our first child last year, and things couldn't be better."

"I notice that Leesburg hasn't changed much since I left almost five years ago. Do students still hang out at the local watering hole like I did?"

"Oh, you mean Charlie's? According to some of my students, it's still a happening place on Fridays and Saturdays. Not sure how things might change next year, though."

"Not sure what you mean, Bob. What's going to change?"

"Effective, the first of January next year, the drinking age in Kentucky is no longer eighteen. It will be twenty-one to meet the national standard set by Congress earlier this year."

"Wow, I guess some things do change quickly. I forecast a lot of underage drinking next year."

Before I inundated Bob with more questions about the detachment, I thought it best to review the ROTC detachment's standard operating policies and procedures (SOP). I pulled the large loose-leaf binder from our shared bookcase.

"Geez, Bob. I never thought ROTC duty would have so many protocols and procedures!"

He wryly responded, "I recommend you put aside some time later this afternoon to go over it. Most of the binder contains our protocols for 'extra duty." Something I suspect you didn't think was included in a ROTC assignment."

Bringing Home the Cost of War

After a quick lunch at home with Alene, I sat at my new desk and opened the thick binder that contained all the SOPs for the ROTC detachment. The table of contents had many familiar sections. Two, however, were unfamiliar and immediately caught my attention. The first, Next of Kin Notification, or NOK Responsibilities, outlined how the detachment met the requirement to provide Department of Defense notification to the next of kin of soldiers killed or who died on active duty. The sterile words immediately prompted me to wonder who and how the next of kin of my soldiers were notified when they were killed in action. As I read the prescribed script and protocols, it became clear that this was a solemn responsibility undertaken by the officer assigned. I wondered how many of these assignments were made during the year and how many would come my way.

The second section, Survivor Assistance Officer, or SAO Responsibilities, provided great detail on how the assigned Survivor Assistance Officer (SAO) would assist the surviving family member(s) of soldiers killed or who died on active duty. Underlined twice was the admonition that the SAO and the NOK officers were never the same. I immediately flashed back to the times I had to identify the bodies of some of my soldiers killed in ongoing combat. I cannot imagine how traumatic it would be for family members when that notification was made, and the awful association they would have with the officer making the notification. I suppose I was naive and had always assumed that somebody else, somewhere, was responsible for these tasks. I never expected to have that responsibility.

Bringing Home the Cost of War

The roster of the detachment officers for duty as Notification of Next Kin or Survivor Assistance was on the bulletin board in the main office. All officers were encouraged to read it frequently and, when assigned next up on the roster as a NOK, be prepared to leave within two hours of receiving the death notice. The NOK officer would then brief the oncoming Survivor Assistance officer once the notification of the next of kin was made. I made a mental note to ask Bob about his experience with NOK and SAO duties.

On the way home that afternoon, I reassessed my assumptions about ROTC duty. Teaching classes and having the same time off as the students seemed like a cushy assignment. Being away for two months each summer and then assigned to NOK and SAO duties was not something I expected. Then again, when had an Army assignment ever provided what was expected?

The following two weeks passed swiftly. The delivery of our household items from storage, putting up curtains and shelves, and buying additional furniture consumed any time away from the office. As our first home, Alene and I enjoyed the challenges of finding just the right piece for the living room or the required number of dinner plates in case we had company. I never tired of watching Alene, intently looking over a catalog, circling numbers, and then smiling when she found what she liked. In the office, I spent time reviewing and revising previous military history lesson plans and refreshing my knowledge of the subjects I would teach. Cadre returned to the office from summer camp two weeks before classes began, and I had the opportunity to get to meet the other officers and noncommissioned officers. What surprised me most was the diversity of branches. My office mate was in air defense artillery, the deputy PMS was from the Quartermaster Corps, a couple of the upper-class instructors were Field Artillery, and even another infantryman. I had the opportunity to speak with two officers who had not attended summer camp and had performed multiple NOK and SAO duties for the detachment over the summer. Each was thankful to be off the NOK and SAO duty roster for a while. When I asked about those duties, each shared their thoughts on making them less stressful, whether for the NOK, a single event, or the SAO, which often involved many days and possibly even weeks. Each said that the NOK duty was the most stressful, but the SAO duty was always the most demanding.

The university required mandatory instructor courses for all new faculty. As a member of the ROTC detachment, I was an assistant professor. The two three-hour courses were taught by faculty from the School of Education and covered everything from syllabus preparation to the university's adopted grading program. I found the time spent worthwhile, as it helped refresh my understanding of how the university expects its faculty to perform in the classroom. All new instructors in the ROTC detachment were required to present their syllabi and class outlines to the senior instructors and the PMS. After presenting my materials and delivering my first four classes, I was approved to proceed.

Bringing Home the Cost of War

My first military history class was on the first Wednesday of the semester. I was probably overprepared because the fifty minutes passed, and I had only completed half of the lesson plan. I quickly realized I enjoyed teaching. My energy level was high. I couldn't explain it, other than that I am certain this is something I am going to enjoy. As I walked back to my office, my feet were at least twelve inches off the floor. The high I felt was soon deflated when I saw Bob's face.

"Another NOK! This is the second one in two months. If I never have to do one of these in my life, it will be too many!"

"Bob, I was going to ask about NOKs. What makes them so bad?"

"For one thing, Jim. You are delivering the worst news a wife, a mother, or a father will ever get in their lifetime. For another, you drop in, deliver the bad news, and then leave. Some other poor bastard has to clean up the mess you dropped on the family. So, NOK is a one-time bad experience for the guy that delivers the notification, but sometimes the SAO follow-up is worse. Sorry, I gotta leave, Jim. Sergeant Jenkins and I are on the clock."

With that, Bob was out the door. Leaving me with many questions.

The eight officer instructors in the detachment were divided into two sections, with four teaching first- and second-year students and the other four teaching juniors and seniors. I rarely had a chance to talk to those teaching the upperclassmen and spent my time with the other three instructors, my office mate Bob being one of them, in my section. As the semester progressed, I noticed that my name was slowly creeping up to the top of the duty roster for NOK and SAO duties. Unsurprisingly, toward the end of the semester, the admin officer called me at home on Saturday morning and told me to come to the detachment for an NOK assignment. After grabbing a quick coffee, I told Alene I would be gone for the day. Over her coffee cup, she asked,

"Is this a notification of next of kin? You told me that this was one of the extra duties performed by the detachment."

"It is. I'll see how it goes. Most other officers have said the first one is the toughest."

"As always, Jim, you will do your best. I love you."

"Thanks, babe. I love you, too.

Chapter Three: The First Notification

A two-member team, an officer and a noncommissioned officer, performed all NOK and SAO duties in the detachment. The Army recommended that a chaplain also accompany the NOK team. However, we had no chaplains near us and none available close to where the notification would take place. I arrived at the ROTC detachment before nine and was happy to learn that Master Sergeant Baker would be my partner for my first NOK assignment. Baker was the longest-serving non-commissioned officer (NCO) in the detachment. He had picked up one of the detachment's military sedans and joined me for a review of the NOK packet that the Department of Defense (DoD) had faxed to the ROTC detachment.

We learned that the next of kin was the wife of a soldier killed twenty-four hours ago in Vietnam. She lived in the town of Wilmington, about thirty miles away. I grabbed the binder with the policies and procedures for NOK duty before we walked to the olive drab military sedan parked outside the ROTC offices and left for Winchester.

As Baker drove to Winchester, I reviewed the protocols for NOK and memorized the specific words required by the Department of Defense. Over and over, I said to myself,

"On behalf of the Secretary of the Army, I regret to inform you that your husband, Specialist Four Jerome Harkins, was killed in action in Con Thien province, South Vietnam, yesterday, the 15th of November."

Master Sergeant Baker, the seasoned veteran in every respect, provided some encouraging words after I put aside the binder.

"Don't worry, Captain. As much as possible, stay professional and everything will work out."

Within an hour, we arrived at the address listed for Mrs. Jerome Harkins. The house, situated in an older, well-maintained neighborhood, boasted a wrap-around porch and a meticulously maintained lawn, with late-fall flowers blooming along the sidewalk. Baker had spent most of the time since leaving campus telling me about other NOK assignments he had had over the past two years. To me, they all seemed sterile and perfunctory. I hoped this first one would be that way. I was in no way prepared for any great drama. My nerves were on edge, my palms sweaty as I gripped the folder of material I would leave with the widow.

Exiting the car and adjusting our uniforms, we walked side by side down the sidewalk to the porch. Our feet barely touched the porch when a male voice somewhere on the other side of the screen door said loudly,

"Get off my porch."

Momentarily taken aback, I replied,

"Sir, I am Captain James Foster, and I am here on official business. Is Mrs. Jerome Harkins at this address?"

Again, the same voice, now closer through the screen door,

"I said, get off my porch."

The words were punctuated by the twin barrels of a shotgun pushed against the screen.

Baker and I did an about-face and walked slowly back to the car. Once seated, I turned to Master Sergeant Baker,

"Well, that was unexpected. What do we do now?"

"Not to worry, Sir. I have had this happen once before, although not with a shotgun. We find the local sheriff and explain why we are here, and he will escort us back to the house where the notification can be made."

It took another two hours to locate the Sheriff, and then an additional fifteen minutes to follow him back to the house listed as Mrs. Jerome Hawkins's address. When we arrived, the Sheriff went ahead onto the porch, opened the screen door, and spoke with someone inside. Then the Sheriff opened the screen door and said,

"They are ready for you, fellas. Jerome's daddy was mighty upset when you showed up. When he saw that green car, he knew why you were here, and he couldn't handle it. Jerome's wife, Linda, is in the kitchen with the Harkins. She has been living with them while Jerome has been away. Her parents passed away a long time ago."

After seeing the shotgun at the screen door, I didn't know what to expect as we walked through the neatly arranged house to the kitchen. It was a scene I would never forget: a comfortable, blue-themed kitchen straight out of the 1940s, complete with Formica tabletop and light blue vinyl chairs. At the table, a young woman, whom I assumed was the wife of the soldier, was sobbing uncontrollably. A visibly shaken older couple stood on either side, attempting to console her. The older man and woman were silent in their grief. I took a deep breath and walked over to the young woman. Peering into her grief-stricken face, I asked,

Are you Mrs. Jerome Harkins?

When she nodded, I delivered the rehearsed, dreaded speech,

"Mrs. Harkins, on behalf of the Secretary of the Army, I regret to inform you that your husband, Specialist Four Jerome Harkins, was killed in action in Con Thien province, South Vietnam, yesterday, the 15th of November."

Without thinking, I added,

"The nation's condolences are with you today."

Both women exclaimed, "No, no, no," while sobbing loudly. It was all I could do to keep my composure. I knew I had to share more information with the widow. I waited what felt like a long time, but it was probably only a minute or two. Once the widow and the soldier's parents regained some composure, I stood awkwardly in front of them. When they realized I still had more to say, they turned their tear-stained faces to me while I briefly explained the role a Survivor Assistance Officer would play over the next month. I placed the folder of materials the Army provides to next of kin on the table and told her that the officer would call her within a day to address her questions and needs. Although not part of the official notification protocol, it seemed right to do one more thing.

I stepped back, stood at attention, and gave the grieving widow my best salute. With that, Master Sergeant Baker and I softly closed the screen door and left the house. As we returned to the car, I was emotionally shaken in a way I had not expected. Why hadn't I known that the Army required us to make notifications like this? Why weren't we prepared in some way to deliver these terrible messages? These thoughts and many like them swirled through my mind as Baker turned the car around to return to campus.

On the way back to campus, I sat uncomfortably in the passenger seat. Suddenly, beads of sweat rolled down the sides of my face as Baker told me I had done well and hoped the SAO wouldn't have any issues with the family. He also mentioned that it was the first time he had a weapon pointed at him, despite many other NOK assignments. I barely heard him, and I felt I hadn't handled the notification well. In a moment of clarity, I wondered what the standard was for performing an NOK. I was physically and emotionally exhausted by the time we pulled into the parking area for the ROTC detachment. No one was in the offices this late Saturday afternoon, and I was grateful for small favors. I figured my appearance would reflect the emotional toll I was under. As I returned the binder to the administrative office, I noticed it was now smeared with the sweat from my palms. My drive home must have been automatic, because I don't remember leaving the office or arriving home.

As soon as I was in the door, I told Alene I needed to shower and change before I could tell her all about my first NOK assignment. After taking off my uniform and a quick shower, I sat down with her and shared the details of this first NOK assignment. When I described the response of the wife and parents of the soldier killed yesterday, she gasped.

"Jim, that's what it would have been like if it were you! I would have been at Mom and Dad's house. That poor woman, thank God she has family to help her."

I did not tell Alene how emotionally drained I felt after leaving the Harkins family. I think she could feel it. Later, I flashed back to when we lost a soldier in combat; we all had an immediate feeling of anguish and a twinge of failure. These feelings were short-lived because the mission was always present, and the needs of the remaining soldiers took precedence. The wounded and dead were quickly evacuated, and their absence was noted, but it had little immediate impact on the unit. The operational tempo of the war provided little time for memorial events and even less for holding a special remembrance ceremony. I remembered clearly the only one I experienced during my two years in Vietnam. The memorial ceremony, while important to all of us in the unit, was a temporary event. We remembered those we lost, but that memory was tucked away. We had our mission. I realize that the way the NOK event introduced death into a family was destined to be long-term. It shattered the dreams and hopes embodied by a husband and a son. The cost of war had landed squarely in that kitchen for the Harkins family.

Alene and I talked until almost midnight. I knew she was doing all she could to help me come to grips with what I had experienced. The house seemed cold and too quiet once Alene went to bed. I thought a few strong whiskeys before bed might help me relax, but they didn't work. I woke up multiple times that night, my nightmares becoming more vivid. Some of them featured Alene and the soldiers I had lost during both deployments to Vietnam. In one particularly intense scene, I saw Alene watching me while I crawled away from a grenade blast that had bloodied my left arm and killed my radio telephone operator next to me. The experience felt so real that I woke up drenched in sweat. I was grateful that Alene was a sound sleeper; I knew my terrors were often loud.

I awoke late on Sunday and drove to the detachment to meet with Captain Barry Tate, who was assigned as Mrs. Harkins' survivor assistance officer. A good part of the conversation was to tell Barry that the soldier's parents would be with Mrs. Harkins, and he should include them in all his meetings. They were her support. When he asked me how the notification went, I told him about the shotgun in the screen door and the demand that we get off the porch.

"Whoa, I haven't had a weapon pulled on me." He exclaimed.

"What did you do, Jim?"

"Thankfully for me, Master Sergeant Baker had a similar situation, but without the shotgun. We found the Sheriff, explained why we were there, and he escorted us back to the Harkins' house. After that, I guess it went as well as could be expected. Both parents and the wife were in the kitchen when I made the notification. They were as grief-stricken as I have ever seen anyone. I gotta ask, Barry, does it get easier?"

"Not really. You become somewhat detached from the actual notification and treat it like a duty assignment you had to fulfill. Every family is different, and every notification and SAO is different."

That Sunday night, as we watched the evening news together, I noticed Alene watching me more closely than usual.

"Jim, something is bothering you. What is it?

"The news is always all about what's happening in Vietnam. I can't help it, but some of the pictures and newsreels affect me more than I can explain."

"What type of effect?"

"I can't explain it very well, but it's similar to what I felt when I made the next of kin notification yesterday. I am nervous, my hands are sweaty, and I feel anxious. It's as if something is going to happen, and I have no idea what it is."

"Is there anything I can do to help?"

"Sweetheart, just being here is all the help I need. I can't imagine what I would do if I felt this way and was all alone."

As she put her arm in mine and lay her head on my shoulder, she softly replied,

"Jim, I am here for you. Tell me what I can do."

"I can't tell you much, sweetheart. Just be here for me, I'm gonna get over this, one way or another."

Chapter Four: The First Survivor Assistance Duty

My name was the first on the SAO roster within a month. My office mate, Bob Schindler, was the next of kin notification officer in Hagard, Kentucky. Bob's return on Wednesday and his debriefing of his NOK duty were, as he described it, a unique experience for him. I couldn't imagine what it would be like for me. According to Bob, the mother of the soldier killed did not know that the soldier had married a young woman shortly before he left for Vietnam. The young woman, who Bob thought was probably no more than seventeen, through her tears begged Bob not to tell the soldier's mother that he had been killed because she would probably kill her if she knew they were married. Bob agreed that he would not contact the mother. Unfortunately for me, this first SAO assignment promised to be a real challenge.

On Thursday morning, I called the number Bob provided for the widow of Private First Class David Johnson. The voice that answered the phone was not that of a young woman. A little confused, I provided my name and asked who I was speaking with. The woman replied, "I am Davy Johnson's mother. Do you Army fellas, have anything to tell me about my son?"

"Ma'am, if Beverly is available, may I speak with her?"

"I learned you soldiers came to her yesterday. She told me that my Davy is killed. Is that true?"

"Ma'am, I can answer your questions once I have talked to Beverly. Is she there?"

Shortly, the voice of a young woman came on the line."

"This is Beverly."

"Mrs. Johnson, I am Captain James Foster, your survivor assistance officer. May I come to your home and provide the information you need as the widow of Private First Class David Johnson?"

Almost breathless, the young woman blurted out,

"I had to tell Mrs. Johnson that Davy was killed in Vietnam. She don't understand why they told me instead of her. I tried to tell her Davy and me was married, but she won't listen."

"Mrs. Johnson, I won't tell you what to do. It is your decision if you want Private Johnson's mother to be present when I visit. If you have other family available, you may wish to have them present."

"I ain't got no family here in Hagard. All my family's down in Colland and they ain't likely to come up here for any reason."

"Mrs. Johnson, I will be at your home tomorrow morning at 11:00. Is your current address 225 Carter Street in Hagard?"

"Yes, sir. That is my apartment that Davy and me rented out after we was married. The rents paid to the end of the month, but I got no money for next month's rent, and I got no place to go."

"I will see you tomorrow."

I now have two issues to deal with before leaving for Hagard. How to deal with the mother of the deceased soldier and how to expedite payment to the surviving spouse. Major Jeb Plank, the detachment's administrative officer, should have some answers. A quick visit to Plank's office provided the assistance needed. I must have evidence that the marriage took place and that Beverly Johnson, nee Hatfield, was the legal wife of Private First Class David Johnson. Should Private Johnson's mother contest the marriage, I can do nothing. Additionally, DoD has a provision for the widow of a soldier killed in combat to receive an immediate death payment. In this widow's case, she qualified, and I obtained a wire transfer from the Finance and Accounting Office in Indianapolis that afternoon. Armed with a copy of the Army documents verifying the marriage and a check for $1,000 for the widow, the next morning, Staff Sergeant Connors and I headed to Hagard. It was a good three-hour trip that gave me a chance to review the procedures for a Survivor Assistance Officer.

After arriving at the address I had confirmed with Mrs. Johnson, I walked up the stairs of a relatively new apartment building to the second floor. I was greeted at the door by a young woman who introduced herself as Beverly Johnson. The small apartment that Mrs.

Johnson rented was neat and clean. An older woman, whom I assumed was Private Johnson's mother, was sitting stiffly in a chair. My introduction was met with a curt nod. I outlined all the matters that I would assist the widow with, including the military funeral and obtaining the benefits due to a surviving spouse. After I told Beverly Johnson all I could and asked if she had any questions, the mother of PFC Johnson demanded that he be interred in the family graveyard outside Hagard. The young widow immediately agreed. She was more than thankful for the check and surprised to learn that she would receive a considerable amount from the Servicemembers' Group Life Insurance (SGLI) Plan that Private Johnson had signed up for shortly after their marriage. Her tears and sobbing after learning about the life insurance were testimony to the effort that Private Johnson made to ensure his young wife was monetarily supported should he die. The look on Private Johnson's mother's face was difficult to understand. I couldn't tell if she was happy for the widow or displeased that the insurance wasn't coming to her. Looking back on that first meeting with Beverly Johnson and the mother of PFC Johnson, it was somewhat anticlimactic. At the time, Private Johnson's mother appeared to have accepted that her son and Beverly had married before he left.

The following two days were spent coordinating with the Funeral Home in Hagard, selected by the family, and arranging for the pallbearers and salute details from Fort Hamilton, the nearest military post. Once the family had decided on the date and time of the funeral service, I accompanied the burial detail to the funeral home to load the flag-draped casket and followed it to the church for the service.

The funeral service was conducted in the First Baptist Church of Hagard on a grey December morning. The weather seemed to mirror the appearance of the attendees. Grey, somber, and sorrowful. A large group of Private Johnson's friends, primarily high school classmates and family, attended, but the young widow had no representation from her family. Surprisingly, the soldier's mother embraced her young daughter-in-law during the funeral and acknowledged that her son had married her. To me, seeing that apparent reconciliation as an expression of shared grief that a mother and a wife never forget. The pallbearers and firing squad from Fort Hamilton did their jobs well, and attendees thanked me for the dignity of the service.

The drive back to Leesburg was a reflective opportunity that I did not relish – how were my soldiers who had died in Vietnam received in their home communities? I hoped that none of their families had experienced the drama I had seen unfold. This was another memory scarred into my mind—one with a strange consequence.

Later that night, when I recounted the funeral, Alene said that the reconciliation between the mother and wife was something women understand and will almost always do. It just takes some of them longer. I was surprised by how Alene explained that. Unfortunately, it didn't help with the nightmares. The latest one was worse, as I saw Alene as the grieving widow and some of the soldiers I had lost as pallbearers. The two drinks after dinner didn't seem to take the edge off the dream any more than the two I had just before bed. Alene had noticed I was going through my prized bottle of bourbon faster than ever.

She looked hard at me,

"If this goes much longer," she said, looking me in the eye, "You and I will have to address it."

I have found getting up in the morning much harder lately. The schedule of preparing my lessons, teaching, and then completing the NOK and SAO assignments after action reports was disruptive, and I no longer made my morning run. My office mate, Bob Schindler, was his usual cheery self on one dreary December morning. Still in his Army sweatpants and shirt, he asked me when I was going to run with the cadets. I responded,

"Bob, I just feel like shit all the time. Running with the kids just doesn't seem the thing to do."

"Well, buddy, a little PT helps with most anything. Tell me when you are ready, and we will take those 'kids' on."

The exchange with Bob seemed to take another bite out of my confidence. That lack of confidence began to show in the classroom. By the middle of the Spring semester, cadets were no longer eager and enthusiastic about my classes. I was more withdrawn. Where cadets had often come to me after class, I withdrew, and they noticed. While I noticed, but didn't think much of it, Lieutenant Colonel Max Duncan, the Deputy Professor of Military Science, did. Before he took his concerns to Colonel Hewitt, he called me into his office late one afternoon.

"Jim, I monitored a couple of your classes, and you don't seem as enthusiastic about your instruction as you were last semester. Is there something I need to know about?"

"No, sir. I think I have just overreacted to the NOK and SAO assignments. I am sure that they won't impact me as much once I have done a few more."

"Jim, I reviewed your files, and you were in some of the biggest firefights in both tours. You were wounded twice as a platoon leader and once as a company commander. You spent thirty days in the hospital recovering. Are you sure you have recovered?"

"I have, sir. I don't think my physical condition is an issue. Seems I am having a hard time adjusting back to the civilian world."

"I can understand that, Jim. You aren't the only one having difficulty returning to the civilian world. Tell me if you need help. I will keep you off the NOK and SAO rosters until you inform me otherwise. OK?"

"Yes, sir. Don't worry, I will sort out this transition. And please, leave me on the roster. I don't want to make the other guys take my place."

"Ok, Jim. But I need to know you can handle it."

Bringing Home the Cost of War

I left Duncan's office feeling an unease I had never experienced. I knew I wasn't as exuberant leading classes as I thought I would be. But to have the Deputy PMS tell me I wasn't doing the job was a wake-up call. So far in my career, I have never had a senior officer tell me I wasn't accomplishing the mission.

For the next three weeks, I paid more attention to my teaching and became almost as engaging an instructor as I had been at the beginning of the school year. Toward the end of the Spring semester, I felt I had recovered fully from the doldrums that had hit me months earlier. The second NOK, just before the semester ended, did not help.

Chapter Five: The Challenging NOK

On Friday, May 15th, I was called at home early in the evening. Major Plank alerted me that, as the NOK on call, I had a notification to make the next morning. I grabbed a quick breakfast and left the house with a cup of coffee in a travel mug. I reviewed the fax from the Department of Defense and assembled the information packet for the next of kin. Two hours later, Saturday morning, Staff Sergeant Sanders and I headed south to the rural countryside east of Midvale, Kentucky. Sanders and I had no trouble finding the listed address on a rural route. It was an unusually warm day for mid-April, and the two-hour trip passed quickly. As we pulled up to the large two-story house, a ten- or eleven-year-old girl left the porch swing and ran to the car. Before we could say anything, the little girl quickly asked,

"Hey, Army guys, my brother is in the Army. Do you know Jamie Whitaker?"

Sander and I exchanged short looks, recognizing that Specialist Four James Whitaker was the soldier we had come to notify the next of kin of his death. I replied to the little girl's question.

"No, ma'am, I don't know your brother. There are many men in the Army that I don't know. I need to speak with your parents. Are they home?"

"They are out at the far barn," as she ran to the car and jumped into its back seat. "Come on, I'll show you how to get there."

Bringing Home the Cost of War

Although I was hesitant to take the little girl along, it was the best way to get to the family quickly. We were thankful for her directions as the multiple rough roads would have been difficult to follow without them. Soon, we pulled around a corner of a large barn, where a man and a woman stood, distributing feed to the waiting cattle. As the car approached the barn, the woman sat slumped on one of the feed sacks along the back wall of the barn. The man dropped the bag he was emptying and stood motionless. Once the car stopped, Sanders and I walked to the couple, with the little girl preceding us.

"Mommy, Daddy, these Army fellas need to talk with you."

I approached the couple and gave my prepared speech.

Mr. and Mrs. Whitaker, on behalf of the Secretary of the Army, I regret to inform you that your son, Specialist James Whitaker, was killed in action in An Hoa province, South Vietnam, yesterday, May 14th. On behalf of all service members, the Secretary sends his condolences."

Before I finished, both parents appeared catatonic. Mrs. Whitaker seemed to have fainted. Mr. Whitaker sat down speechless and unmoving. Just then, Sanders exclaimed,

"Sir, the little girl has run off down the road. I can't see where she is going."

I was at a loss. I had worked hard to maintain a professional bearing and hold in my own emotions, and now we had two completely unresponsive parents and a little sister who had run away.

And we are in the middle of nowhere. I tried asking Mr. Whitaker if he had anyone they could call to have them come to the barn. He was completely unresponsive. After the third or fourth attempt to get any response and before Mr. Whitaker responded, a pickup truck roared up to the barn with the little girl in the passenger seat. The young man driving jumped out of the truck and immediately ran up to Mr. and Mrs. Whitaker.

"Mom, Dad. Peggy just told me that Jamie was killed. Let me help you get back to the house. Guys, can you give me a hand?"

With our help, the young man was able to load both his parents into the pickup, with the little girl riding in the back. Sanders and I followed in the olive-drab Army sedan. When we returned to the farmhouse, the two parents were helped to their bedroom. The young man introduced himself as we waited in the front room of the house.

"Jamie was my younger brother, and Peggy is my little sister. My name is Walter. Is it true that Jamie was killed in Vietnam?"

"Yes, sir. I received the confirmation last evening, and we were directed to make the notification within twenty-four hours. I have additional information for your parents. Do you think they can give me a few minutes? I won't take long, as it is more informative than anything else."

"Let me check. Mom is lying down, and Dad is still pretty much in shock."

When he returned,

"Mom is pretty much out of it, and I don't think Dad could take much in. How about you tell me what they need to know, and if I have questions, I can call you."

"Certainly. Walter, your parents will soon receive a call to set up a visit from an officer assigned as their Survivor Assistance Officer. His role is to assist with all the necessary steps after the service member's death. Based on their decisions, he will arrange the funeral details, including the salute squad, casket, and all required supporting documents. Unfortunately, there are many administrative procedures, and the Survivor Assistance Officer will help them manage them. I recommend you be available to support your parents once the Survivor Assistance Officer has scheduled the appointment with them. You should expect a call within the next day."

"I understand. I live just down the road and will be here for Mom and Dad. Let me give you my telephone number, as well. The officer can always call me."

"Thank you, Walter. I will make sure the Survivor Assistance Officer knows to keep you in the loop."

We said our farewells and left through the front door. I saw the young sister crying quietly on the porch swing as we walked to the sedan. She looked up at us with a strange expression of bewilderment tinged with anger. I immediately thought about how the siblings of any of my soldiers might respond when they learned that their brother had been killed. A sobering thought that lingered long after we returned to campus. This was going to be an interesting NOK after-action report. Since it was late evening, I called the designated SAO, Captain Jackson, and we decided to wait until Sunday morning for me to debrief him on the NOK. As the assigned SAO for the Whitakers, Jackson would need to know all I could provide.

As I recounted the experience with Alene later that night, I kept seeing the face of little Peggy Whitaker. How happy she was to help us find our way to her parents, how sad she looked as we left. I knew I would see that sad face repeatedly in my nightmares. I hoped that the family surrounding them would support Jackson's role as SAO for the Whitakers. Within the week, the nightmares returned with a vengeance.

Alene mentioned more than once that my temper was getting worse. She said she wasn't sure when I was going to go off on some little thing. Her admonitions did little to help; I continued to feel like I was losing control.

The end-of-semester break had been a relief for me and the rest of the detachment, even though two officers had to perform NOK duties close together. I was thankful that I was no longer near the top of the NOK roster. However, the SAO roster was another matter, as I was called to Major Plank's office not long before the end of the Spring semester.

Chapter Six: The Different Assistance Assignment

"Jim, you are the next up for an SAO assignment. Here are the details. You and Staff Sergeant Jacobs will be doing the honors."

I reviewed the Department of the Army message to find that an officer from the local recruiting station had notified the next of kin. I called the number listed for the officer and had a helpful conversation.

"This is Captain Jim Foster at Southern Kentucky University. Is this Captain Steele? I am the SAO for the Jackson family. Can you give me a debrief on the family?"

"Jim, George Steele here. I have only done one other NOK, and that was in town here in Wilmington for a guy who died in an automobile accident. This was my first for a soldier killed in combat. The Jacksons live in a very rural area outside Jonesville. The roads in that area are not great, so take it easy. The family seemed pretty stoic and showed very little emotion when I gave them my spiel. They have been told you are coming, and I have a telephone number for you to call them.

My first phone conversation with the father of Specialist Jackson was brief. I learned that the local funeral home was the designated recipient of the body and that the funeral service would be held in the family church sometime in the next two weeks. Besides that information, the father replied that I could come as soon as I wanted.

It all seemed perfunctory to me, but I now recognized that each family processed their grief differently. Staff Sergeant Jacobs and I made plans to leave the next morning. The plan was to visit the funeral home and then the family. Once the funeral details were finalized with the family, Staff Sergeant Jacobs would contact the staff at Fort Hamilton to arrange for the pallbearers, bugler, and firing party.

Arriving at the funeral home in Jonesville, I was struck by the ornate front and large sign announcing, "Fitzhugh Funeral Home." Upon entry, the man who greeted us was a dead ringer for Washington Irving's Ichabod Crane character. Tall, thin, and pale, Mr. Fitzhugh was dressed in a black three-piece suit, black tie, and white high-collar shirt. If I ever imagined what a funeral director would look like, this is him.

After Fitzhugh showed us into a small room, he quickly looked around without further discussion and said,

"Captain, you will find the Jackson family a bit different."

"How so, Mr. Fitzhugh?"

"The Jackson family has been around these parts longer than any family, it's been said. The story is that the original Jacksons came here and settled this part of Kentucky early on. They came here with some strange customs, and when someone marries into the family, they adopt those customs."

"How will that affect our role as the Survivor Assistance officers?"

"Among other things, you won't meet any of the women. The men are very protective, and the women are rarely seen. The church they established way back when is attended only by them and a few close friends. They have little or nothing to do with the church or the people here in town. Unless you are introduced to any of the women in the family, I suggest you deal only with the men."

"I thank you for that information. It will help us assist where we can. Have you received confirmation on the date Specialist Jackson's body will be here?"

"I have, and it should be within two or three days. I have also learned that it will be a closed casket. I will call you once he has arrived."

I spent the next few minutes reviewing the funeral service procedures. Fitzhugh had not supported a military funeral and admitted this was all new to him. I was surprised that he did not know a firing team would provide the twenty-one-gun salute before the bugler played taps. Fitzhugh told me the family would be digging the grave, and no outside groups were allowed in the graveyard. I realized that a site visit to the church was necessary, as Fitzhugh had only a rough idea about the building and the gravesite.

"Thank you, Mr. Fitzhugh. I appreciate all the information. I look forward to your call."

The trip to the Jackson family home was everything and more than Captain Steele described. The gravel road often became no more than a dirt road with deep ruts where vehicles had carved out the track. The Jackson home would have fit nicely in an 1800s painting. The single-story log cabin, with its full-length front porch, was characteristic of the cabins of early settlers. Sergeant Jacobs drew my attention to the four other log cabins, which were within three or four hundred yards of the Jackson home, closest to the road. When Jacobs and I walked up the path to the front of the house, we were met by a group of six men on the porch. Each of the six had a full, well-groomed beard and wore dark pants held up with suspenders, along with a light blue shirt. I belatedly realized that these were almost uniforms. Unsure as to exactly which one was the father, I directed my introduction to what appeared to be the oldest of the six.

"Sir, I am Captain Jim Foster, and this is Staff Sergeant Jacobs. I am the Survivor Assistance Officer for the family of Specialist Jesse Jackson."

"You are expected, Captain. My brothers will be with us. Please come in and sit at the table."

The interior of the house, or cabin, was as rough as the log walls. A few shelves were the only signs of any domestic activity. The long table that dominated the room was a carpentry work of art. Intricately carved crossbeams supported wide planks that glowed with age and care. The deep chairs around the table were additional evidence of the carpenter's exceptional skill. The following two hours were spent with me explaining the benefits provided by the Army to the family members. I confirmed that the Funeral Home would receive the casket and that it would be a closed casket. Once the family decided on the date and time of the funeral service, we would arrange for the military support. I spent some time detailing how the funeral service would be organized, from the pallbearers placing the flag-covered casket in the church to the final playing of taps after the 21-gun salute. I noticed that some men looked strangely at each other when I mentioned the gun salute, but I didn't think anything of it at the time. It was the only break in their stoic demeanors. The mention of the insurance payment elicited the briefest of nods from Mr. Jackson, but nothing more. As Jacobs and I were preparing to leave, I asked if he had any questions.

"No, Captain. I think I understand all that you have given us. We will let you and the Funeral Home know when we will have the service for Jesse."

I asked where the church is located so that we can help prepare military support for the funeral service. Mr. Jackson hesitated for a moment before responding.

"When you return to the road, take the right fork at the first junction. The church is close by on the right. We will conduct the service, and you won't have to do anything inside."

The church was easy to find. Its whitewashed walls sparkled in the early afternoon sun. I immediately recognized it as a beautiful example of early American construction—small, compact, and befitting of the countryside. The door was not locked, and Jacobs and I walked in. The center aisle was narrow with a row of pews on either side. I estimated that the church could likely hold fewer than fifty or sixty people in the five rows on either side. The pallbearers would have to squeeze the casket in after everyone was inside. There would be no room with the rows of benches extending to the walls.

The long ride back to Leesburg was punctuated by observations from Staff Sergeant Jacobs that I had missed.

"Captain, didn't you think it strange that we saw no women in the house while we were there? The soldier's father's five brothers probably live in the other log cabins we saw nearby."

"Come to think about it, you're right. Usually, both the father and the mother are present. It's only been forty-eight hours since they were notified, and she may be with other family members. I didn't hear anything about any brothers or sisters of Specialist Jackson. There weren't any pictures of Specialist Jackson or other family members anywhere. There wasn't anything on the rough walls that I could see."

Two days later, I received a call from the Funeral Home that the body of Specialist Jackson had arrived and was prepared for burial. The family had opted for the casket that the Army provided and insisted that the funeral director let the Army conduct the funeral. The funeral director waited for the family to tell them when the funeral service was planned. The funeral director said they had never had a military funeral in the community, and he was grateful that I was handling that part. Rather than waiting for the family to call, I called the family on Thursday and asked when they planned to have the funeral service.

"The funeral for Jesse will be held on Sunday next at the chapel. We are preparing his grave in the family plot next to the chapel. The service is for noon on that day." Replied the father.

Staff Sergeant Jacobs contacted the Fort Hamilton office responsible for providing military funeral support and confirmed we would meet the party at the courthouse in Jonesville at 10:00 am on Sunday. Jacobs and I arrived at 10:00 on Sunday to find a fifteen-passenger van parked in the courthouse parking lot with a group of soldiers waiting around it. I was greeted by a young sergeant who explained that the pallbearers had rehearsed for a few days, and the bugler was an old hand. He had just rounded up the seven who would serve as the firing squad, but was confident, as they had done funerals before. I first noticed that the pallbearers were all over six feet tall, blond, and blue-eyed. "My first thought was that the eight pallbearers must have all been from Minnesota. How did the Army match up this crew?"

After we arrived at the Funeral Home, I placed the flag on the casket, and the pallbearers carried it into the hearse. The hearse followed us and the van to the chapel. We arrived at 11:30, and to my surprise, no one was outside the chapel to greet us. We now had ample time for Jacobs and me to show the firing party and the bugler their locations. I put the bugler up a slight rise about twenty yards from the open grave. Sergeant Jacobs led the firing party around the back of the church with instructions to move to the right of the bugler once the casket approached the gravesite. My briefing to the pallbearers was succinct.

"There is a very narrow aisle in the chapel. The first two pallbearers will precede the casket on the trolley provided by the funeral home. There is not enough room for the pallbearers to accompany the casket on either side. Two others will follow the casket and push the trolley provided by the funeral home to the front of the chapel. The remaining four will stay outside the church until the service is completed. I will give the order to raise the coffin. Any questions?"

The young soldiers looked a little uncomfortable. One raised his hand.

"Captain, that is not how we rehearsed. Are you sure?"

"I am. The pews in the chapel extend to the walls, and the center aisle can't be more than three feet across. There is barely enough room for two people to walk in, much less two with a casket between them."

"I understand, sir. We will do the best we can."

Within minutes, the chapel's front door opened, and one of Mr. Jackson's brothers, whom I had met earlier, approached.

"Captain, the prayer service has ended. We can begin the service for Jesse as soon as you are ready."

Bringing Home the Cost of War

Staff Sergeant Jacobs and I, the young sergeant in charge of the burial party, straightened our uniforms and moved to our positions. The funeral director brought the trolley to the front door of the chapel. The pallbearers removed the flag-draped coffin from the hearse, carried it to the chapel's entrance, and placed it on the trolley. I nodded to the family member who had opened the door, and the pallbearers proceeded through it. The two lead pallbearers quickly moved to the front of the casket, and two others fell in behind. The remaining four pallbearers stood on either side of the entrance at parade rest. The flag-draped casket filled the aisle, and the four pallbearers did an about-face to the door of the chapel. I stood at the entrance, with the pallbearers facing me. I watched as another, I assumed, Jackson family member moved to the front of the chapel. While he did, I looked around the chapel. The men were on one side, and the women on the other. The family member began to speak in an accent that I could not understand. Soon, a rhythmic humming came from both sides of the aisle. This was closely followed by exclamations from both the women's and men's sides of the chapel. Before I could take in what I was hearing, I suddenly saw both men and women falling to the church floor. Looking at the pallbearers, I saw four pairs of eyes growing wider as the cries and falling bodies increased. Mouthing "Stand fast," over and over, to the four pallbearers, I thought, "This is something none of us has ever experienced. Good Lord, what happens next?"

Bringing Home the Cost of War

While it may have seemed longer, the congregation recovered within minutes. The family member leading the service moved forward, laid his hand on the casket, and delivered a silent prayer. I recognized that this was the end of the service and gave the command, "Recover." With that, the two pallbearers in front moved the casket on the trolley to the church's entrance. The remaining six then flanked the casket and followed me around the side of the chapel to an open grave less than ten yards away. The newly dug grave was covered with slabs of freshly cut wood. I walked past the grave, turned to the pallbearers, and watched as they carefully placed the flag-draped casket on the slabs. I watched approvingly as the eight pallbearers performed the flag-folding ceremony, and the last pallbearer would pass the flag to me. While the flag was being folded, I looked for the family members to whom I would be presenting the flag. I recognized Mr. Jackson and noticed that the men and the women were no longer segregated. An older woman dressed all in black now stood next to Mr. Jackson. The senior pallbearer presented the flag to me, saluted, and marched the pallbearers to the side of the crowd. As I walked toward Mr. Jackson and the woman next to him, the two stepped forward. I stopped in front of the two, extended the folded flag, and said,

"On behalf of the President and a grateful nation, please accept this flag as a token of the sacrifice made by Specialist Jesse Jackson." Each reached for the flag; momentarily, each held on. Abruptly, the woman took the flag and pulled it to her breast. Mr. Jackson did not look surprised.

The passing of the flag signaled the firing party to begin. I heard the sergeant begin the sequence, and the first volley, then the second, and finally the third, echoed in the woods. I looked around and found that only those in uniform were still standing. Everyone else was either lying flat on the ground or kneeling. Many winced as the final volley signaled the end of the twenty-one-gun salute to the fallen. As the bugler played taps, I saw much brushing of dust from pants and skirts. More than a few in the crowd looked chagrined. I flashed back to my reaction to rifle fire not so long ago and guessed that many in attendance had been fired upon before, and their reactions were understandable.

The sergeant in charge of the burial party marched the soldiers to the waiting van. Staff Sergeant Jacobs and I waited until all those attending the funeral had approached the casket, placed a hand on it, and left. After there was no longer anyone else at the grave site, Mr. and Mrs. Jackson walked up to me. Still clutching the folded flag, Mrs. Jackson looked at me.

"Young man. Can you tell me that my boy didn't die for nothin?"

Taken aback by the question, I was surprised and struggled to decide on a response. I finally decided.

"Ma'am, when your son and I joined the Army, we wrote a blank check to our country that included our lives. All I can say is that your son served honorably. Today, we honored that service in the best way we could."

Mrs. Jackson nodded, turned, and walked away, followed closely by Mr. Jackson.

As they walked back to the waiting burial party, Staff Sergeant Jacobs turned to me,

"Captain, I have done more than a dozen military funerals in my career. This one takes the cake for being the strangest. The question Mrs. Jackson is probably one that every mother wants to ask. She is the first one that I have heard ask the question."

The grave site was now a small flurry of activity as family members placed ropes under the casket and removed the planks above the grave. Slowing and deliberately, they lowered the casket into the grave. After throwing the ropes into the grave, they shoveled the dirt pile alongside into the hole that was soon filled.

Debriefing the burial party was a standard practice, and I made sure that the team, especially the pallbearers, knew what a good job they had done. One of the young soldiers' comments captured their expressions during the service.

"Captain, I had no idea what was going on. It seemed everyone suddenly had a fit. I was afraid we might have to start CPR on someone."

"It was a surprise to me, too, but you did well, and I will make sure the folks at Hamilton are reminded of that."

Bringing Home the Cost of War

The trip back to campus was unusually quiet as Staff Sergeant Jacobs and I processed the events of the last few hours. That evening, as I described for Alene the funeral service and the strange behavior of the attendees, she offered that she had heard about religious groups called "holy rollers" who probably acted that way in a church service. I did not share with Alene the question from the mother that I tried to answer. My answer and the look on Mrs. Jackson's face when she asked that question lingered in my mind more than I care to admit. The nightmares are not getting better, and how many times I awaken during the night is getting to be a problem.

Alene also noticed significant changes in me. The most disturbing to her was my depression and volatility. Sometimes I would be angry at little things, which was difficult to understand. Alene appeared unsure about how to address those outbursts that were happening more often. She tried setting up romantic dinners and even purchased incense that promised "soothing thoughts and quiet contemplation." None of which seemed to make any difference.

Chapter Seven: The Challenging NOK

The end of the Spring semester was encouraging for me. The classes I taught were among my favorites during my time in ROTC, and I had looked forward to teaching a new group of cadets. Unfortunately, I was not exercising enough, and my uniform told me I needed to lose weight. The nightmares were ever-present, as was a continual feeling of being out of sync with my environment. I couldn't seem to relax, even when Alene and I took a short vacation over spring break. Never patient with poor drivers, I alarmed Alene with my reactions to some of the "idiot drivers" I cursed on our way to the hotel in Macon. When we returned to Leesburg, I promised Alene that I would cut down on my drinking and start running again. The next NOK assignment immediately put aside that promise.

I was called to the administrative office during the final week of the semester for the next NOK assignment. When I looked at the fax from the Department of Defense, my heart sank. Specialist William Brooks, Headquarters Company, 505th Parachute Infantry Regiment, was a name I immediately recognized. That recognition struck hard because Brooks was my company's medic. I knew Brooks well, and the notification process for a soldier that I knew brought back the memories of our time together in the jungle and some of the brutal fights we both endured. As the company commander, I knew my troops well and often learned about some of their personal lives and families. The NOK notification fax confirmed what I already knew:

that Brooks was married and Linda Akins Brooks was the surviving spouse. Her address in Steward was within a forty-minute drive.

Sergeant First Class Hoskins had the detachment sedan ready and met me in the parking lot. On the way to Steward, I talked about Specialist Brooks and how he had supported the company in Vietnam as the company medic. More than once during the drive, I flashed back to the time that Brooks treated me when I was slightly wounded during an intense firefight. I recalled the thin, black man with gentle hands who said, "I gotcha, Captain. Ain't nothing but a scratch. I'll have you bandaged up and back in the fight most skosh." To infantry soldiers, the medic was the one they looked to whenever they needed help. From insect bites to bullet wounds, the medic was there for them. I could not help but wonder how Brooks was killed.

The bright spring day didn't help my apprehension. As we pulled up to Mrs. Brooks' address, I almost wished I had passed on this NOK. The knock on the door went unanswered, and repeated knocks were also unsuccessful. No car was in the driveway, and none was parked in front. We looked at each other and realized we were going to have to find Mrs. Brooks another way. Sergeant First Class Hoskins saw a neighbor watching them and suggested that he ask if the neighbor knew where Mrs. Brooks could be. After a brief conversation, he returned and reported that the neighbor knew Linda Brooks and said she was visiting her parents in Ruth, a small town east of Steward, and would likely return in a day or two.

We checked our road map and left for Ruth, Kentucky. We were quickly running out of time and decided that contacting the Sheriff would help them find Mrs. Brooks quickly in such a small town. The sheriff's office was quickly located, and we were greeted by an elderly African-American who introduced himself as Sheriff Jonah Marshall.

"Sheriff, I am Captain Jim Foster, and I have to contact Mrs. Linda Brooks."

"I guess you are looking for Linda Akins. She married the Brooks boy about three years ago. Am I right?"

"Yes, sir. We are looking for Mrs. William Brooks. Do you know where we may find her?"

"This is a small community, Captain. I know where Linda's family lives, and I can take you to it."

"Thank you, Sheriff. That saves us a lot of time and probably wasted effort."

A short drive ended at a white bungalow, which the sheriff identified as the Akins' residence. Repeated knocks on the door went unanswered. I turned to the Sheriff,

"Are there any other relatives that Mrs. Brooks may be visiting?"

"Loretta Akins has some cousins back in Steward, but I don't know where they live. I can give the Sheriff in Steward a call and see if he can help."

"Thanks, Sheriff, but I am concerned that our effort to contact Mrs. Brooks might alert too many people. I can tell you why we need to see Mrs. Brooks, but can you keep it between you and the Steward Sheriff?"

"I can guess you are going to tell Linda that the Brooks boy has been killed in Vietnam?"

"Yes, sir. That is our mission today, and the sooner we deliver the bad news, the sooner the Survivor Assistance Officer can help the family."

"I don't envy your task, young fella. Let's get back to my office and see if we can track down Linda Brooks."

Over the next two hours, Sheriff Marshall and the Sheriff in Steward were able to track down three relatives of the Adkins. With three addresses, I had a difficult decision to make. Calling at the three addresses gave them a thirty-three percent chance of Mrs. Linda Brooks being there. The first address was the closest. A young woman greeted Sergeant First Class Hoskins and me as she left the house.

"May I help you?" She asked.

"Yes, Ma'am. I am looking for Mrs. Linda Akins Brooks. Do you happen to know where she is?"

The young woman looked uneasy as she answered, "I do. Linda is my cousin. She and her mother are visiting my aunt Beth three streets over."

"Is that 218 Mayburg Street?"

"Yes, it is. May I ask why you need to find Linda?"

"Ma'am, I am afraid I just need to talk with her. That is all."

Hoskins and I walked quickly back to the car. We assumed that a phone call from the young woman would likely alert the family members that they were on their way. As we approached 218 Mayburg Street, we saw the expected telephone call had been made. A young woman, about twenty-two, was standing on the porch. Dressed casually in slacks and a white blouse, she stood stiffly waiting for us to exit the car and approach the house. I walked to her and asked,

"Are you Mrs. William Brooks?

Quietly, she answered, "I am."

"I am Captain James Foster. Mrs. Brooks, on behalf of the Secretary of Defense, I regret to inform you that your husband, Specialist William Brooks, was killed in action yesterday in An Long Province, South Vietnam. The entire Department of Defense extends condolences on your loss."

With those words, the young woman's face collapsed. She looked at me, "I know who you are. I thought you were taking care of Billy." With those words thrown at me like darts, she turned quickly and rushed into the house. I knocked on the door and was greeted by an older woman who looked like a mature version of the young woman I had just delivered the worst news a spouse can receive. The woman looked hard at me.

"What more do you need to do, young man?"

"Ma'am, I need to inform Mrs. Brooks that she will shortly be contacted by an assigned Survivor Assistance Officer who will help her through the administrative tasks she will face. May I do that?"

"Young man, there is no need. I will tell my daughter what she needs to know."

"Yes, ma'am, I understand. Do you have a good telephone number I can provide to the Survivor Assistance Officer so he can make arrangements to come and support Mrs. Brooks?"

"We will go on back to Ruth in the morning. Here is the number at the house. He can call there."

"Thank you, Mrs. Adkins. When you think it appropriate, please tell Mrs. Brooks that I served with her husband and feel his loss deeply. Specialist Brooks was our company medic, and everyone thought the world of Doc Brooks."

"I shall tell her later," replied Mrs. Adkins as she quietly closed the door on me and Sergeant Hoskins.

Hoskins was silent on the drive back to Leesburg. I felt utterly drained from the day's efforts to locate Linda Brooks and deliver the awful news to her. This was the one NOK I wished I had never been assigned. As I dozed on the trip back to campus, I flashed back to the many times I watched Doc Brooks take care of the company's soldiers. Doc Brooks was always there, from minor skin infections to major wounds from enemy action. The continued reminder that the soldiers

I lost in two years in combat probably had the news of their deaths delivered much the way I had delivered it today. As much as I tried to keep disassociated from the delivery of the death notification, this one was for a soldier that I knew, and knew well. The sense of loss and grief was almost too much. That night, when I told Alene about the notification, I broke down crying while telling her about Brooks.

"Alene, this is the guy who cared for us all. He was our medic. When I was wounded, it was Doc Brooks who bandaged me up and gave me the good news that it was not serious. I can see his face right now. Christ, why didn't I get someone else to do this one?"

I am sure Alene had never seen me so emotional. The other NOK assignments had always unsettled me, but this was at another level. In retrospect, her compassion led her to be concerned that I might be having more emotional issues than she ever imagined. She now suspected that my increased drinking might be a symptom of a problem that she had never experienced and had no way to address. She told me later that she thought of calling her mother and asking for her advice, thinking that if her father had anything like Jim did, she might be able to suggest some help.

"Jim, we have been married for such a short time. How could I have misunderstood you?

On my part, I couldn't shake the feeling of dread that I had following the notification of Doc Brooks' wife. Why was I so down?

Even the few intimate moments with Alene didn't have the same flavor. What the hell was going on?

My distraction carried over to my classes. Before I knew it, I was behind in grading the papers the freshmen had turned in last week, and the end-of-semester exams were just around the corner. Classroom time, something I had enjoyed so much at the beginning of the year, now seemed to drag on. I dreaded preparing for each class, showing up for class, and going through the fifty minutes without losing my cool over some stupid question from a student. Unfortunately, my distraction did not go unnoticed. Just before leaving on Friday, the PMS asked me to come to his office.

Before I was sitting in the chair next to his desk, Colonel Hewitt looked hard at me.

"Jim, I can see you are having problems. Is everything all right at home?

"Everything is fine at home, sir. I can't explain why things seem to sour lately."

"I know the last NOK was for a soldier you served with during your last tour. How did it affect you?"

The thoughts of that meeting with Doc Brooks' wife brought an emotional response that was totally unexpected.

"Sir, Doc Brooks was my company medic. Hell, he was the one who took care of all of us in the company. He was even the first one I saw after getting hit by that mortar round. He was an essential member of the company. I was unsure how I would feel about making the notification until I had a chance to think about it afterward. Tracking down Mrs. Brooks added to the drama, and her response made it feel like it was my fault."

"I am sure that was a tough one. I also understand that you could have deferred it. Why didn't you?"

"Right now, I think I felt it was my duty to make the notification because Doc Brooks was a member of my unit, and I would want someone close to me to make it for my wife. I am not sure that was the best decision."

"Jim, let's get through this semester. I am going to put you on the summer camp training team so that you won't be pulling NOKs or SAOs this summer. Take some time off this Spring before heading up to summer camp. Spend some quality time with your wife and try to decompress from the NOK and SAO experiences."

"Yes, sir. Sounds like a plan. Thanks for listening."

I knew I had gotten off easy. I don't think the colonel knew how bad things were. I am sure my colleagues teaching the underclassmen knew I wasn't pulling my weight. I suspected that some of their students who were also in my classes were expressing their disappointment. So far, only one colleague, my office mate Bob Schindler, has given an indication. Initially, he offered to help in some of my classes.

"Jim, are your classes going well? My reason for asking is you seem to be struggling with some of them."

"It seems like this semester was tougher than the first. It could be a different group of students. Some are unhappy about having to take ROTC. It's still mandatory for all males to take the first two years of Military Science, but some aren't happy about that, and their attitudes mirror that."

"It's one of our challenges. Your prep seems a bit shorter than last semester. Is it harder?"

"I'm not sure what you mean, Bob? I still seem to have leftover material every class."

"Jim, I don't want to give you a hard time, but I have heard Steve and Charlie, the other two instructors in the underclass instructor group, indicate your students are having a hard time."

Chapter Eight: A Classified Notification

Just before the end of the Spring semester, I was next on the NOK roster. I knew it would be the last one before the summer break and my trip to summer camp in Pennsylvania. On Sunday evening, I received a call from the admin office that an NOK fax had just been received. I had my uniform ready, and within thirty minutes, I was in the ROTC office reading the fax. This one was unusual for two reasons. First, it was Sergeant First Class Roscoe Richter. All my other NOKs had been young men, seldom old enough to be a sergeant. Second, the fax was classified as CONFIDENTIAL. I had never had a classified notification. I called Lieutenant Colonel Duncan and asked if this was something I needed to handle differently. His somewhat ambiguous response was,

"Jim, it can mean one of two things. It can mean that the soldier was on a classified mission, and where he was killed cannot be listed. Or, it could mean that the soldier is being considered for the Medal of Honor, and the family is not to be advised of that until the President approves it."

His response didn't provide much information, as I would have conducted the notification in the same way. The only difference I could see was that the standard notification language did not include a general location in the country where the soldier died. It merely stated, "...in the Republic of South Vietnam."

The newest noncommissioned officer in the detachment, Staff Sergeant Peters, would be my partner for this one. He had pulled the olive drab sedan to the front of the building, and after reading the fax, said we could leave when I was ready. The address provided for Mrs. Robert Richter was just north of Leesburg on the outskirts of Ledward, Kentucky. It was less than a forty-minute drive, so I suggested to Sergeant Peters that we grab a cup of coffee at the all-night diner on the way out of town. I did not want to arrive at the Richter residence too early on a Sunday morning and, if the wife was going to church, catch her either before or after.

While we drank our coffee and ate a donut, Sergeant Peters asked several questions about the notification.

"Captain Foster, how many of these have you done?"

"This is my third."

"Are they hard to do? I haven't ever done anything like this in my seven years in the Army."

"I can say they are hard, but not physically. They are hard because you are telling a family that it is destroyed. The husband, son, or brother they knew is gone. You are going to experience some of their grief because you are delivering that ending of the family."

"I never thought of it that way."

"Sergeant Peters, I noticed that you are not an infantryman. What is your MOS?

"Sir, I am a 91B, a wheeled vehicle mechanic."

"You did serve a tour in 'Nam?"

Yes, sir. I was stationed at Nha Trang. We took care of all the vehicles of the 4th Transcom, the guys that supplied most of I and II Corps."

"Did you lose anyone in your unit?"

"We lost two guys from my section who went out on a vehicle recovery. They were ambushed."

"Did you ever wonder how their families were notified of their deaths?"

"No, sir. Come to think about it, we had a little ceremony for them, but after that, I don't think we thought much about them."

"Well, what we are going to do in the next hour is to make the death of a husband, and possibly a father, a permanent part of this family. We try to do it as professionally as we can with as much empathy as possible. We are just the bearers of the bad news. The SAO will help the family for the next days, weeks, or months it takes to satisfy all the administrative bullshit the DoD requires."

The trip to Mrs. Richter's address took less than thirty minutes. We arrived close to 10:00 am. Ringing the doorbell and knocking on the door did not result in anyone being home. Sergeant Peters asked,

"What do we do now, Captain Foster?"

"We wait."

Bringing Home the Cost of War

I had Peters pull around the block out of direct line of sight of the house, but with a clear view of the driveway. Just after 11:00, a car pulled into the driveway, and two children, probably eight and ten years old, piled out of the car and ran to the front door. A woman left the car and opened the front door of the house.

"Ok, Peters. Pull up to the house, and let's make the notification."

We stepped out of the car and walked to the front steps, where we were met by the woman we had seen leaving the car in the driveway.

"Good morning, gentlemen. What's going on?"

"Ma'am, I am Captain James Foster. Are you Mrs. Roscoe Richter?"

"I am. What's going on?"

"On behalf of the Secretary of the Army, I regret to inform you that your husband, Sergeant First Class Roscoe Richter, was killed in action yesterday, May 12, in the Republic of South Vietnam."

"Oh, no. There must be some mistake. My husband is stationed in the Philippines with the 7th Special Forces Group. He would have told me if he was going to Vietnam. There has to be some mistake."

"Mrs. Richter, I am sorry, but the official Department of Defense Casualty System just doesn't make mistakes like this."

"Oh, God. What happened?"

"Ma'am, we don't know. A survivor assistance officer will contact you within one day. He may be able to answer your questions.

I have a folder that you and that officer will need. Please accept our condolences. Is there anyone you would like us to contact for you?"

"We just got back from church and Sunday School. Could you contact the Pastor at the First Episcopal Church in town? Let him know what happened and ask him to come by. I have to take care of our children. I don't have time for anything else."

"Yes, ma'am, we will do that right away."

As we headed back to the car, Sergeant Peters asked,

"Captain, do you think this might be a mistake? Maybe another Richter was killed?"

"Sergeant Peters, I doubt the Army would screw this up. How many Sergeant First Class Roscoe Richters could there be in the Army?"

We found the First Episcopal Church and were told by someone in the church that Father Roberts was in the rectory at the back of the church. I left Peters in the car and knocked on the door. When a middle-aged man answered the door, I assumed he was the Pastor.

"Father Roberts, I am Captain James Foster, and I just notified Mrs. Roscoe Richter that her husband died in Vietnam yesterday. She asked if you could come to her house."

"What a terrible time she must be having. I will go to her immediately. Is there anything you can tell me that might help?"

"Father, we don't have much information. A survivor assistance officer will be supporting Mrs. Richter and should be contacting her within a day. I suggest you speak with him as soon as possible. Do you have a telephone number I can share with him?"

"Here is my number on the back of this card. Please instruct the officer to call me at any time. Young man, you look exhausted. May I assume that these notifications are difficult for you?"

"Father, as much as you try to detach from the news you are delivering, it never gets any easier. Initially, Mrs. Richter thought there was some mistake because she had no idea her husband was in Vietnam. That was a first for me, and it kind of threw me for a loop."

"Bless you, young man. I do not envy your job. I will leave for Mrs. Richter's immediately."

Peters and I drove back to campus without a word. Just before he dropped me off at the ROTC building, he turned to me,

"Captain, are these NOKs always like this?"

"Sergeant Peters, sometimes they are a lot worse."

At dinner that night, Alene was quieter than usual. I felt she needed to say something after I told her about the Richter NOK. She didn't, however, and it wasn't until after we had cleared the table that she sat down next to me on our new couch. She placed her hand on my arm.

"Jim, something is wrong. I want desperately to help you. The drinking is out of control and, quite honestly, you look terrible."

"Alene, I don't know what to tell you. This last NOK was as stressful as any of the others. It seems like just as I think I have squared myself away, things go haywire right off the bat."

"Is there anyone you can talk to? Anyone who has any experience with what you seem to be going through?"

"I can't think of anyone at the detachment. Colonel Hewitt took me aside a couple of weeks ago and suggested I take some time off. If I do that, I am acknowledging that it's something I can't handle. I'm not ready to do that. I'll get a grip on things once the semester is over."

I have finally finished grading the last of the semester's exams. I didn't see any happy faces on my students when I returned their exams. I admit I am a tough grader, but this time I hit them harder than before. I was disappointed in their performance, yet I felt a little guilty for not giving them all that I once felt capable of providing in my instruction. I also realized I was withdrawing from my classroom instruction. That realization hit home when students stopped coming to my office hours. During the Fall semester, I often had one or two freshmen at my door. I even had a couple of seniors who were looking to branch into infantry as their first choice. As the only infantry officer on staff who had served in both platoon leader and company commander roles, they sought my thoughts on their future as infantry officers. Since the beginning of the Spring semester, there have been no cadets visiting during office hours. Was I getting to be that much of a pain in the ass? As we were putting away our slides and textbooks for the end of the school year, I asked my office mate,

"Bob, be straight with me. Have I become a real asshole this semester?"

"OK, I'll try. You are not the same guy who started last Fall. I don't know what has changed you, but sometimes you seem angry about something, but never let on what that is. More and more, you seem withdrawn. You may not have noticed, but you and Alene haven't attended any of the parties we've had in the last three months. Doris and I invited you two over for dinner weeks ago, and you didn't respond until I asked you point blank, 'You coming over, or not?' Your uniform was always in great shape. Now, it seems you have lost all interest in wearing any awards and decorations. The plain green uniform is all the students see."

"Jesus, Bob! Am I that bad?"

"After every NOK or SAO, you seem to get worse. I am not surprised the Colonel offered you the chance to get off the roster."

"How did you learn the Colonel offered that?"

"Come on, Jim. It's common knowledge among the officers. You are a wreck after each NOK, and the SAO assignments don't seem much better."

"I never expected to have the NOK duties affect me that much. Try as much as I can, I still can't get rid of the flashbacks to losing some of my soldiers. The thought that their families experienced the same thing I introduced to the families I am assigned makes it even harder. Believe it or not, I am looking forward to spending time at summer camp, no NOK or SAO duties."

"I hope you are right, Jim. Summer camp with the cadets can be a daily grind that doesn't give you much time for anything else."

When I told Alene that I would be at the ROTC summer camp for a month, she seemed almost relieved.

"Jim, this will be a great time for me to spend some time with my folks in Columbus. Mom has asked me more than once when we were going to visit. I think it is also a good time for us to figure out how we are going to deal with the issues that keep cropping up more and more."

"What issues do you mean?"

"Come on, Jim. You're drinking more than ever. Your nightmares have turned into insomnia, and you are withdrawing from me more and more each week. I don't know what's wrong; I can't seem to help you, and honestly, I'm worried that our marriage isn't what we both expected it to be."

"Come on, Alene. It can't be that bad!"

"Maybe from your perspective, it isn't, but from mine, it is."

Taken aback, I sat there with my second drink of the evening, unsure of what to say. It was clear that both my wife and my coworker were concerned about me as I spiraled downward, yet I felt unable to reach out for help. Where do I go from here?

Chapter Nine: ROTC Summer Camp and Help?

A week later, I was on my way to Indiantown Gap, the location for the ROTC Advanced Camp for cadets from all over the East Coast. I learned that for the second consecutive year, the 82nd Airborne would provide the support troops for the camp. Although they were not from my brigade, seeing the maroon berets was a bright spot in what was otherwise a pretty grim post. The bachelor officers' quarters (BOQ) were located in an old wooden barracks that had not seen better days since World War II. My room was made primarily of wooden wallboards, with cracks large enough to let in the sunrise across my rickety cot. Even if I had wanted to sleep in, my roles in various field exercises required me to be up early, often before sunrise, to prepare for the day's events.

On the first Sunday, I decided to attend the church service conducted by one of the 82nd chaplains. The old chapel wasn't in much better shape than my BOQ, but the wooden pews could probably tell many stories of the soldiers who occupied them over the years. The chaplain was a tall, angular man with an accent that hinted at a Boston upbringing. For some reason, after the service, I felt compelled to stick around and talk with him. Out of his chaplain's vestments and dressed in his fatigue uniform, I noticed he was wearing a 173rd Airborne shoulder sleeve insignia on his right shoulder. To those unfamiliar, this insignia indicated that he was a combat veteran from the 173rd Airborne Brigade, a unit with a long and storied history in Vietnam.

"Chaplain, do you have a minute?"

"Sure, I'm Jack Marshall, and even though I am a Catholic priest, we hold nondenominational services when with the troops."

"Jim Foster, I have been assigned to the Southern Kentucky University ROTC detachment. Right now, I run the night tactical course and the land navigation course."

"I noticed that you are an 82nd veteran. Were you in the Golden Brigade in Vietnam?"

"I was. I served as the company commander of Bravo, 2nd of the 505th, '68 and '69."

"Well, Jim, I was a little before that. I was a platoon leader in Alpha Company, 1st of the 503rd in 1966 and 1967."

"Jack, were you ever in the Central Highlands? I was a platoon leader in the 3rd Brigade, 25th Division, 1966."

"We probably overlapped at some time because the 173rd did operate in the Central Highlands while I was there. I was wounded and medevaced in early '67 while we were up in Kontum Province."

"It's a small world, isn't it? Did you get back to your platoon?"

"No, I spent a few weeks in Japan and then went back to the States. My last year on active duty was as a training officer in a Basic Training Brigade at Ft Hamilton, Kentucky."

Before I could say anything else, he continued,

"Jim, let's grab some lunch at the Brigade mess hall and catch up on what it was like with the 82nd in Vietnam."

"Thanks, Jack. May I meet you there? I have a couple of things to take care of before lunch."

"Sure, see you there around 1230?"

"I'll be there."

As I made my way to the makeshift office that I shared with two officers from the supporting battalion of the 82nd Airborne, I considered talking to Chaplain Jack Marshall about the flashbacks, insomnia, and general feelings of apprehension that were troubling both me and Alene. I wondered if he experienced similar issues. If he did, how did he manage them as a chaplain? Since he had served as a platoon leader and was more seriously wounded than I was, I was curious about how he transitioned to becoming a chaplain and what motivated that change.

I saw Jack talking to a couple of soldiers at the entrance to the mess hall. He was clearly well-liked. The paratroopers talked easily with him, and he joked with them in a way that illustrated how comfortable he was in his role. I didn't want to seem like I was eavesdropping, so I approached and asked.

"We still up for lunch, chaplain?"

He turned, smiled, and said goodbye to the two soldiers.

"Sure enough, Jim. My treat."

As we made our way through the chow line, I watched how Jack interacted with the cooks and those serving the meal. The ease with which he was able to make them smile and respond to his questions about their unit, their families, and how they liked Pennsylvania gave me the confidence I needed. Once we found a place to sit together, Jack opened the conversation.

"Jim, I can't help but notice you seem to want to ask me something. What is it?"

"Jack, I don't know where to start, but I'm having some problems, and I thought you might be able to help me. Over the past year, I've been assigned as a Next of Kin (NOK) notification officer for four soldiers killed in Vietnam. When I returned from my second tour, I didn't expect to have any problems adjusting. However, each NOK notification, as well as the SAO duties, seems to intensify my nightmares and general unease. Have you had a similar experience?"

"Let me ask, is this affecting your work and your family? I see you're wearing a wedding ring, so I assume you're married."

I am, and my wife, Alene, is worried. My responses to her concerns aren't helping. My teaching is suffering. I've already been counseled twice by my detachment commander, and I'm really at my wits' end."

"I believe you mentioned that you've been wounded more than once. If that's the case, I assume you've seen your share of heavy combat and lost some soldiers. Am I right?"

"Yes, and the NOK notifications seem to trigger more and more memories of those I lost in my platoon and company."

"Jim, it's important for you to know that you are not alone. Many of us who returned from combat have gone through similar experiences. While there is no quick fix to stop the pain, there are new approaches that can help. I am an example of one of those approaches. I faced challenges that were just as difficult as yours shortly after returning home. My time in the hospital in Japan may have worsened things because I witnessed some severe cases, and sadly, several patients in my ward did not survive."

"How do I get that help?"

"First, you need to be clinically evaluated. There is a new term that's now used to describe what was once known as 'shell shock.' It's now recognized as post-traumatic stress disorder, or PTSD for short. My final duty station at Fort Hamilton, Kentucky, was close to the University of Louisville Hospital, where a couple of doctors were working on a VA grant to find ways to treat PTSD. The number of returning soldiers experiencing symptoms like ours is quite large. I was included in one of their study groups, and that's where I received the treatment and support I needed. I don't consider myself cured;

rather, my symptoms are managed in ways I couldn't have achieved before."

I realized that I hadn't touched my food. A glimmer of hope appeared. If Jack had similar problems and had improved, perhaps I could benefit from the same treatments.

"Jack, how can I contact the folks in Louisville? I'm willing to try anything to improve."

"I have the phone number and the name of the doctor I saw. She is great, and I'm sure she would welcome your call," he replied.

"I can't thank you enough. First, for listening to me, and second, for providing a window of support,"

"Don't thank me too soon. Not everyone responds the way I did. I'll pray for your success. In the meantime, I'm always available to listen. Sharing combat experiences with other veterans is one of the coping mechanisms researchers have found to be helpful. You and I probably have more than a few screwups from our time as lieutenants to talk about."

"Absolutely. I'll call Dr. Johnson this week and see what options are available. Thanks for sharing her information with me. If it works for you, could we schedule a lunch date?"

"Jim, right now the Brigade is on a six-week cycle. How about Thursdays for the next month?"

"That sounds great. I look forward to lunch next Thursday."

After a hearty handshake with Chaplain Jack Marshall, I almost ran to the administrative offices to find a payphone. The two on the outside of the building were available. I checked my pocket change to make sure I had enough quarters, dropped one in, and dialed the number of the Louisville Hospital. The operator told me to deposit another seventy-five cents, and a warm voice answered, "Dr. Johnson's office. This is Mary. How may I help you?" I introduced myself and explained how Chaplain Marshall had recounted his experience with Dr. Johnson's trials, and suggested that I call. Her immediate, encouraging response,

"Captain Foster, when can you come into the office to be seen by Dr. Johnson?"

"I am in training in Pennsylvania and will be available in four weeks. May I call and schedule something on my way back to Leesburg, Kentucky?"

"Certainly, we can do that. Is it possible for you to provide an outline of your military experience so that Dr. Johnson can be better prepared? I can give you our mailing address."

"I will do that. What is the best time to schedule the initial appointment? It takes about nine hours to get to Louisville, so I would appreciate an early morning appointment for the next day."

"Just call a couple of days before you leave, and we will set it up then. The outline should be sent as soon as you can, OK?"

Bringing Home the Cost of War

"I will complete that and send it to you as soon as I can. I look forward to the appointment in four weeks."

The following two days were spent struggling to complete and outline my somewhat brief experience in the Army. After all, I had been in the Army for less than five years, with two of those years spent in combat. I assumed that Dr. Johnson would want me to focus on that wartime experience, so much of my recollection was focused on those two years. Those were also the most vivid memories, particularly when I remembered the soldiers I lost during that time. Ever present were the faces of the two lieutenants killed while I was their company commander. When I made an NOK, those faces followed me. I finished writing up all I could, stapled the pages together, and mailed them in a brown envelope to the address provided by Dr. Johnson's assistant. I put my mailing address here at Indiantown Gap and underlined the end date for that address four weeks in the future.

The next four weeks went quickly. My instructor responsibilities were long but demanded less of my attention. The bright spot each Thursday was lunch with Jack Marshall. The long lunches were filled with war stories. Each of us was attempting to outdo the other with the outrageous stories of how we had survived. We each had more than enough stories about the ludicrous events that bring levity to otherwise serious situations. He was genuinely happy to hear that I had made contact with Dr. Johnson and encouraged me to meet with her as soon as possible.

Bringing Home the Cost of War

As I closed out the tactical training events and said farewell to the support troops from the 82nd Airborne Division, I thought about the upcoming visit to Dr. Johnson. The scheduler in her office confirmed my appointment for two days from now. She had probably heard it all from other veterans. I wondered how my experience might be different from theirs. Jack Marshall had not told me much about the treatment Dr. Johnson offered the trial group. I wasn't even sure I would be in a trial group. My hopes were high because I realized I needed help.

Chapter Ten: Is There a Way Out?

The trip to Louisville was longer than I had planned, and I arrived at the downtown hotel after 5:00 p.m. I had been given an 8:00 am appointment with Dr. Johnson the next day at the hospital annex, four blocks away. A quick breakfast and a fast walk to the annex on a bright August day should have buoyed my spirit. A tingle of apprehension lingered in the back of my mind. What if she has nothing to offer, and I continue this downward spiral?

A pleasant greeting from the young woman at the small desk complemented the well-decorated office space I entered.

"Good morning. How may I help you?"

"I'm Jim Foster. I believe I have an 8 o'clock appointment with Dr. Johnson."

"Oh, yes. Captain Foster. Welcome to Louisville. Dr. Johnson will be out to see you in a minute."

Almost immediately, a brown haired woman of an indeterminate age opened the door behind the desk and approached. She smiled,

"Captain James Foster, I presume? I am Shirley Johnson.

"Yes, ma'am. Thanks for getting me in so early."

"Please join me in the office, and we will get down to work. I assume you want to get home to your family as soon as possible."

As I followed Dr. Johnson into her office, I noticed that it wasn't like any doctor's office I had ever been in before. It was more like a family room or private club room. No overhead lights. Soft lighting from lamps placed around the room. Upholstered chairs are arranged around an oversized coffee table that holds a thermos and two coffee cups.

"Captain Foster, how about a cup of coffee? I have a little coffee shop around the corner that makes some of the best."

"Yes, ma'am, a cup of coffee is more than welcome."

As I took in the rich aroma of some really good coffee, Dr. Johnson picked up a folder from the coffee table and opened it to the pages I had sent earlier. I also noticed several comments written on the sides of the folder, but I couldn't read them. It was clear she had spent some time reading my information. I hoped that was good news.

"Captain Foster, may I call you Jim? And, please call me Shirley."

"Yes, Shirley."

"Great. Jim, what do you hope to gain from participating in our study?"

She was getting right to the point, and I was initially unable to answer. I stalled for time by taking a couple of sips of coffee, "What can I say that will help? In this case, honesty is probably the best response."

"Shirley, I feel like I am on a downward spiral. I can't seem to communicate with my wife, and my work is suffering badly. It's all I can do some days to drag myself out of bed, and the things that once interested me no longer have any appeal. I am at my wits' end and have no idea what to do."

"Jim, I can't make any big promises, but if you are willing to work, I can promise some improvement. There are a few things I need to know before we consider any treatment. From your notes to me, it appears that your notifications of next of kin trigger you. How does that happen?"

"Whenever I meet the next of kin, spouse, or parent, I think about the soldiers I lost in my unit and how their death notification was made. I strive to be both professional and caring. Still, the act of notification triggers an emotional response in the person receiving the notification that I can't help but feel with them. Even though I have known only one of the soldiers, I seem to know them all somehow. The ones I knew come back each night in my nightmares, and I cannot seem to get rid of any of them."

"How often do you have nightmares?"

"Every night."

"Are you drinking more because of the nightmares?"

"Yes, I drink to sleep harder, but can't. After a particularly heavy nightmare, a good shot seems to calm me down."

"Has your wife commented on your drinking?"

"She has, and it's one of the issues we can't seem to resolve."

"You mentioned problems at work. What did you mean?"

Her calm, almost comforting voice urged me to lay bare my problems. Without hesitation, I responded,

"Everything is going badly. I can't concentrate on my classes, and preparing for each one is difficult. I no longer socialize with other members of the detachment, and I can tell they see me as far less effective than I was a year ago."

"Have you talked to anyone else about this?

"Jack Marshall, who suggested I see you, is the only one I have opened up to. He is also a veteran with many of the same experiences I had."

"That's good news, Jim. One of the activities we have found helpful for veterans is talking with other veterans. We have learned that those who have experienced combat share something that others cannot understand or appreciate. Do you plan to keep in touch with Jack?"

"I do. We have exchanged phone numbers, and he told me I could call whenever I wanted to talk."

"I recommend that you take Jack up on the offer. As a veteran and a minister, he can offer insights not available to others. Let's talk about other methods of coping with your flashbacks and possibly the nightmares. First, I suggest that you have a candid conversation with

Alene. She is your first line of support, and having her fully aware of the challenges you face will provide another layer of support you need. Second, I will provide a summary of our conversation, which I suggest you share with your leadership. I need your permission to do so, but I strongly recommend this because without their acknowledgement of your situation, it will be much more difficult for you to manage the psychological impact you have experienced."

"Did you say psychological impact?"

"I did, Jim. We have learned that intense combat has a significant psychological impact on the individual. Some can ignore it, and others have the impact forcibly awakened by certain events. Some react to loud noises and bright lights. Others, to some degree, like you, find themselves unable to manage the emotional response to the psychological impact that went unnoticed."

"Shirley, I am trying to wrap my head around what you just told me. So, I suffered some psychological impact during my time in combat, and it is now affecting my life."

"Right, and from what you have told me, the performance of notification of next of kin and survivor assistance assignments has triggered that psychological injury."

"So, I suffered an injury that I didn't know about until something I did recently triggered it?"

"I think you understand where you are now. Until now, physicians described what combat veterans experienced as 'shell shock' or 'battle fatigue.' They tended to treat it as a physical injury rather than a psychological one. We now understand that the psychological effects may be more profound than we ever considered."

"Shirley, the two steps you suggested seem only the first of many. What else can I do that might help?"

"There are some medications available that may help. I must caution you that they don't work for everyone. Find a doctor who can help manage the meds and be very aware of how they affect you. One I can prescribe will help you sleep. The other may seem a little out of place, but it helps reduce anxiety and may help you overcome the responses you experience. Unfortunately, we haven't had enough time to work on other approaches to post-traumatic stress disorder. Our focus right now is on behavioral changes that address the symptoms and eventually help the veteran manage the results of the trauma. Unlike physical wounds, psychological wounds never heal. They are simply managed."

"I guess it's something to understand that I'm not crazy. There for a while, I had no idea what was happening to me. Any suggestions as to how I explain this to my chain of command?"

"Jim, I can write a letter explaining my diagnosis. You and your boss will need to agree on what you can and cannot do to improve. Since the NOK and SAO duties seem the most significant triggers, I recommend you be excused from them for a while."

"That won't endear me to my colleagues at work. It will mean they have to pull more of them."

"How many of your colleagues have experienced combat in the way that you have?"

Among the ten officers, there are only two other infantry officers, and one of them hasn't been to Vietnam. The other is too senior and will probably retire soon."

"I would guess, then, that you are the one in ten who has PTSD. You should remember, it's a wound. One that is almost invisible until it begins to destroy your life. We have learned most recently that soldiers with PTSD are ten times more likely to commit suicide."

"Jesus Christ, Shirley! How about the soldiers from my units? They saw as much combat as I did. Could they all have PTSD?"

"They could, Jim. Unfortunately, PTSD manifests differently in each individual. It is clear that veterans from World War II and Korea suffered from it and never received the treatment or care we believe is now available. How did they manage? We aren't sure because those who are still with us appear, at least for the most part, able to manage any PTSD they suffered."

"Shirley, this has been a great help. I will be doing all I can to address my problem. May I call you when I have questions?"

"You certainly may. Please provide the name and address of your commanding officer at the ROTC detachment. I will be sending a letter directly to him with my clinical evaluation. It's up to you and him as to how you will manage your PTSD. I also recommend a long conversation with your wife as soon as you get home. If you have some time, there are a couple of members of the study group that you should meet."

"Absolutely. Alene is not expecting me home before late in the afternoon."

The following two hours were both illuminating and instructional. The first veteran, Charles Bonner, was an infantry squad leader in the 9th Marine Division and was wounded twice while at Khe Sahn. His story was one of survival, both in Vietnam and back in the States. Discharged medically, he wandered for months across the US, never quite sure he wasn't going to commit suicide. When a friend recommended that he see Dr Johnson, he was able to learn how to manage his PTSD. The methods Bonner learned included a physical fitness routine, meditation, and networking with other Vietnam veterans. When I asked if there were any "triggers" that ramped up his PTSD, he responded, "Movies about Vietnam. I trashed a theater once when I was watching Born on the 4th of July."

The second veteran, Joe Stankey, was also an infantryman who served in the 25th Infantry Division in 1966. He married after returning from Vietnam and, in no uncertain terms, described how his PTSD led to his divorce. He, too, was close to suicide after his divorce. He noticed my wedding ring and immediately told me that a frank discussion with my wife was the first thing I needed to do. More bluntly, he said, 'If she can't or won't support you, I don't see much chance of success for you in managing your PTSD."

The two hours passed quickly after we shared some of the more humorous events each of us experienced while in Vietnam. Bonner wished me well as I left. Stankey slapped me on the back after I thanked him. "Jim, remember the good times. Let them become the memories."

Chapter Eleven: Can I Work Through It?

The drive back to Leesburg seemed far longer than the actual two hours. My mind was swirling with what I had learned. I was also trying to work out exactly what I would say to Alene and how the conversation would go. At the moment, she was uppermost on my mind. The meeting I would have to have with Colonel Hewitt was in the back of my mind. Yet, I somehow felt comfortable with that upcoming meeting, probably because Dr. Shirley Johnson had opened a window on something I had no clue about. Could it be the reason for my problems? My only concern was what she would include in the letter and how Colonel Hewitt would react to the letter.

Alene knew I would be home today, so I was not surprised to see her at the door when I pulled into the driveway.

"Jim, I am so glad you're home. How was the drive? When did you leave?"

"I have a lot to share with you, Alene. Let me get my stuff out of the car, and we can sit and I can tell you all about my last few weeks."

I wasn't sure what that look on her face meant. It was a concern, clearly, but also a hint of wariness. Had my behavior over the last months been that bad? The two trips from the car with all the stuff I had at summer camp didn't take long, and we were soon at the kitchen table. A fresh pot of coffee provided the time I needed to settle my emotions. As I looked over my cup, Alene appeared ready to hear of my time away.

"First, let me tell you that the summer camp experience with the ROTC cadets is a good break from the classroom. I enjoyed the assignments I had this summer and met a great group of support troops from the 82nd Airborne. One of the guys I met may be one of the more important meetings I have had recently."

"Well, you now have my complete attention. What was that all about?"

"Jack Marshall, rather Chaplain Jack Marshall, is also a Vietnam veteran and, I believe, he has helped me get on the right track."

"Jim, what do you mean, the right track?"

"Alene, you have seen how I have been over the past six to eight months. I was drinking too much. I was angry all the time, often for no reason. Our relationship was not what it was when we arrived in Leesburg. And, there is a reason for this. Jack helped me understand what I had and what I could do about it."

"Jim, what did he do that was so important?"

"Jack referred me to a program run out of Louisville Hospital that specializes in what is called post-traumatic stress syndrome, or PTSD. According to the doctor there, I have PTSD in a big way, and the NOKs and SAO duties likely triggered it in ways I only now understand. That is why the symptoms did not appear immediately after I returned from Vietnam."

"Oh my god, Jim. What can I, what can we do?"

"First and foremost, we need to understand what PTSD is and what it is not. It is a psychological wound, not a physical one. Unlike physical wounds, PTSD manifests differently in each individual. Mine interferes with my physical well-being, my relationships with others, including you, my love, and often irrational responses to minor irritations. I have to learn how to manage it so that we can live a normal life."

"I almost hate to mention it now, but you haven't been the same person I married almost two years ago. Thank God, you have had it diagnosed. What can I do to help? Are there things we can do?"

"Two things. Just keep loving me as you always have, and tell me when that asshole I've become shows up. Deal?"

The radiant smile that first captured my heart was all the answer I needed.

That evening, as we cuddled on the couch, I shared specific accounts of my work with the cadets over the summer with Alene. The summer camp for the cadets is their first real opportunity to learn what it will be like when they are commissioned. All of the cadre take seriously what we try to accomplish during the six weeks we have the cadets.

My thoughts, as I drifted off to sleep that night, were about my upcoming meeting with Colonel Hewitt. I assumed that the concept of PTSD was as new to him as it was to me. Unlike a physical wound that might require some physical accommodation, how do you accommodate and support an officer with this psychological wound? I guess I would see.

I went in extra early that Monday. I wanted to have a little time by myself in the office before going to see the PMS. While putting away some of my instructional materials from summer camp, I was surprised to see Colonel Hewitt look in the door.

"Jim, it's a nice morning for a walk on campus. Will you join me?"

"Yes, sir. I'll grab my hat."

Our walk down the long stairs to the outside of the building was all about the summer camp and how well our cadets had done. I was able to give him a little review of the cadets from Southern who came through my leadership stations. The Colonel remarked that my evaluations were consistent with those of other school cadres. As we started across campus on a bright August morning, Colonel Hewitt turned to me,

"Jim, the letter from Doctor Johnson didn't surprise me. I noticed you were struggling after the first NOK assignment. I may not have much experience with what she called PTSD, but I know what happens to men who have experienced heavy combat. You realize that you are the only officer in the detachment with a Purple Heart, and you have three of them? The other combat arms officers haven't experienced combat the way you did. Believe it or not, I have seen the effects before. While I was in the 82nd Airborne as a young officer in the 1950s, we had combat veterans who had survived D Day. We had combat veterans who had jumped with the 187th Combat Command into North Korea. All those soldiers had seen more than their share of combat. I also saw that many of them struggled to adjust to a peacetime Army. Not that they weren't good soldiers, but their private lives were a mess. If they were married, many were divorced. Unfortunately, many who left the Army died soon after, at least half by suicide. I think I understand what you're going through. I do not intend to share Doctor Johnson's letter with anyone, but I will work with the senior staff to determine how we can keep you off the NOK and SAO rosters until you and possibly Doctor Johnson believe you are ready."

He stopped and looked at me. "Jim, what do you think?"

"Sir, you just took a big load off my mind. I had no idea how Dr. Johnson's letter would be received, and I thank you for all you have done. I could not ask for more."

"Jim, I believe we have an obligation to those of you who have experienced combat, particularly those whose leadership in combat often made the difference between life and death for their soldiers. We should never forget those who died, but we can't let their memory cause us harm. Now, I trust you will get back to preparing for the Fall semester and teaching the military history courses you did so well last Fall semester."

"Yes, sir. I am looking forward to those classes even more than ever."

With those final words, I saluted and headed back to the office. I noticed that Colonel Hewitt continued his walk and was soon out of sight. It would be an understatement to say that Colonel Hewitt's response was the most positive I could have wanted. I felt that his support would be the foundation for my recovery. Now I had to take the steps Dr. Johnson recommended. A conversation with my office mate, Bob Schindler, was at the top of my list. With the Fall semester still two weeks away, activity around the detachment was slow. Bob had taken a week's leave after summer camp and wouldn't be back until Wednesday. I thought a phone call to Jack Marshall would be helpful, and I could tell him about the positive response from my boss.

I called the number Jack gave me and left a message with his chaplain assistant asking Jack to call when he had a chance. In an hour, my phone rang with the return call from Jack.

"Hey, Jack. How's the 82nd doing today?"

"Good to hear your voice, Jim. How did the meeting go with Dr. Johnson?"

"I think it went well. She educated me on what PTSD is and gave me some things to work on that should help. One of them was to talk with other vets. Do you have a couple of minutes?"

"I do. What's on your mind?"

"Johnson sent a letter to my boss describing what PTSD is and how it affects those with intense combat experience. She also suggested some ways the organization can help. The Colonel had a long talk with me this morning, and I am both encouraged and feel supported. From our conversations, I think he has seen the symptoms of PTSD before and recognized them in me."

"Jim, that's great news. When your organization supports you, it makes your efforts that much more successful. How did it go with the wife?"

"Alene is very supportive, as I knew she would. She wants me to get fixed as soon as possible. When I told her it might be a long haul, she was all in."

"You may want to remind her that you aren't broken and the concept of getting fixed might cause some problems."

"Jack, I think I see that, but how best to help Alene understand?"

"I can't answer that question. I suggest that you remain engaged with your wife throughout the process. If she sees improvement along the way, understanding develops."

"Jim, have you found a veterans group to join?"

"I think I am missing out on this, Jack. The American Legion and VFW here in town are primarily comprised of veterans from World War II and the Korean War. I have learned that Vietnam vets, even active duty like me, are not welcomed with open arms. We are encouraged to join, but it doesn't seem to be a good fit for the older veterans. Some of them are a little dismissive of our service, and, believe it or not, there are fewer and fewer combat veterans in those organizations."

"This is an unfortunate fact of life for us. The veterans organizations across the US seem to mirror your experience. Are there any combat veterans in your organization?"

"I am one of two infantry officers in the detachment. The other spent a year in Korea and has been told that he will probably go to Vietnam within a year or two. None of the other combat arms guys, an Armor officer, and a field artillery guy have been to Vietnam."

"Well, it looks like you may not find a group of Vietnam vets to meet with. You can call me whenever you want to talk."

"Jack, I appreciate it. I'll try not to abuse the privilege. Airborne!"

"All the way, Jim."

Over the next three weeks, I threw myself into class preparation for the Fall semester. One new class focused on leaders of the First and Second World Wars, which had me reading biographies of Marshall, Eisenhower, Patton, and Montgomery. I had almost forgotten how much I enjoyed history. Bob Schindler returned to the office, and he and I went off campus to lunch.

"Jim, this invitation to lunch tells me we have something to discuss. Am I right?"

"Right you are, Bob. I learned a great deal over the summer about why I was acting the way I was, particularly after completing an NOK or SAO assignment. I have been diagnosed with PTSD, or Post Traumatic Stress Disorder."

"Never heard of it, Jim. What does it do?"

"It's not so much what it does, but how it manifests itself. According to the doctor, I shut down my psychological responses to some of the more intense combat experiences while in Vietnam. NOKs and SAOs brought up those responses, and I couldn't deal with them. My reactions included drinking too much, cutting off socially, and putting stress on my marriage."

"One thing is for sure. You weren't the same guy who checked in more than a year ago. I wondered if you were on the downside of a breakdown. Half the time, you seemed pissed off at everything and everybody. The other half, you were somewhere else."

"Bob, I almost want to laugh because you have described the effects of PTSD perfectly. I want to let you know that I am learning how to manage what I have and hope you understand that this is not an overnight fix."

"Never fear, Jim. Please let me know how and when I can assist you. I have some news. The Artillery Branch has just informed me that I am scheduled to deploy to Vietnam in six months. Looks like we'll have Christmas here, and then I'm off. It's been a great two and a half years so far here at Southern. Barbara is even thinking about staying in Leesburg while I am gone."

"Whew, that is news. How did Barbara take it?"

"We expected it because all of our friends from Fort Sill have already been or are going to Vietnam. Any thoughts?"

"One of the things that helped me during my last tour was a support group for Alene while I was gone. Her family and the folks around and at Fort Benning were great. Should Barbara decide to stay in Leesburg, you can count on that type of support for her."

"That is always good to learn. Since I haven't been to Nam, as a battery commander somewhere in Vietnam, can you give me any advice on what to look forward to during that year?"

"Bob, the world of the infantry and the artillery overlap more often than you might think, but the day-to-day decisions you make tend to be the most important for both your troops and the infantry you support."

Bob was quickly all ears as I laid out the things I thought important for him to know. Contrary to much publicized draftee misbehavior, he would soon be hard-pressed to tell the difference between those who were drafted and those who voluntarily enlisted. Identifying and supporting his strongest noncommissioned officers was at the top of my list. As important as our job as commanders might be, we cannot and should not try to do everything. The NCO's role is crucial to the unit's success.

On a more personal note, I reminded him that his artillery positions will be supported by infantry units, often a company from the Brigade or Division. They will see the security duty as a "stand down," or break from humping the jungle. They are your first and only defense against a ground attack on your unit. You might take extra effort to provide them with the extras they don't get in the jungle. Among these are hot coffee in the morning and a cold beer in the evening. If you're having a cookout, invite the infantry to join you. You will never know how much that is appreciated. Often, an infantry company will perform security duty at a firebase for only three or four days. You may be at the same firebase for a month or more, so you will get to meet many different company commanders. Learn how well the artillery support is doing its job. In particular, invite the company's forward observer to spend some time with you. He is the one the infantry company commander relies upon to manage the fire support for the company. There is no other officer who can provide you with the information you need. If it is good news, share it with your NCOs and troops. They need the positive feedback whenever it is available.

Our lunch lasted longer than either of us expected. When I finished my little information session, Bob took a deep breath.

"Jim, that was great. I had no idea that the relationship was as close as it is in Vietnam. I plan to delve into your experience further shortly. You mentioned that you had met with Colonel Hewitt. How did that go?"

"Bob, good news and bad news. He is very supportive and shared that he had met some of the World War II and Korean War veterans with what they called shell shock or battle fatigue back then. Now the bad news. He took me off the NOK and SAO rosters for the next semester, so you guys will come up more often."

"I think we can handle it, Jim. Not to worry. Do what you need to do to manage this PTSD."

Chapter Twelve: Shared Trauma?

My military history class was listed in the History department as an elective that applied to the undergraduate history major or minor. As a result, I often had one or two students who were not in the ROTC program. I tried to address all the students equally, regardless of their ROTC status. It was a slight surprise when one of the non-ROTC students showed up for my office hours one afternoon. All teaching faculty members were required to have at least two hours a week in their office, where students could meet with the instructor. Oftentimes, it was because a student was having problems in the course or just needed additional instruction. Seldom was that visit to complain about a grade. In this case, it was.

Second-semester sophomore and non-ROTC student Jason Grundy knocked on my door and took the chair next to my desk.

"Captain Fisher, I thought I might get a break from a Vietnam vet, but I guess I was wrong!"

"Well, Mr. Grundy, that's an interesting way to start our conversation. Can you tell me why you feel that way?"

"Listen, sir, I am having a hard time in my classes, and I thought I might get a break with an ROTC cadre teaching the course. I understand you are another combat veteran, and I thought it might help me."

"First of all, Mr. Grundy, I didn't know you were a Vietnam veteran. Since you didn't tell me, how could I have helped?"

"Oh shit, I guess that's on me. I was drafted in '67, finished Basic, AIT, and Jump school, and ended up in the 101st in Vietnam in late '68. I got an early out in January of this year, and this is my first semester at Southern. I had two semesters at Northern Kentucky Community College. The classes there were a piece of cake compared to what I am taking here at Southern."

"Jason, who were you with in the 101st?"

"Second of the three-two-seven, First Brigade."

"Well, you just missed me. My company, Bravo, 2-505th, was attached to your battalion for four months in early 1968. Lots of time in the Ashau Valley."

"You're right there. We lost some good guys in the Ashau. I never want to see that godforsaken place ever again."

"So, Jason, what's giving you the most trouble?"

"The amount of reading I have for my history courses is overwhelming. I'm struggling to concentrate, and I find that I miss the key content in every test, including yours, even though I can't recall it. It's frustrating as hell. I am living off campus, so I have all the time I need to study. The GI Bill covers my tuition and fees, as well as a little more, so I don't have to work yet. Do you have any suggestions?"

"Jason, let me ask you a few questions because I don't want to assume I know what you can do until I have these answers, OK?"

"Fire away, Captain."

"Do you have any problem sleeping? Are nightmares recurring?"

"Yes, I have a problem getting a full night's sleep. Workouts and even some drinking don't seem to help. The nightmares are there, even if I can't remember them when I wake up."

"Are you taking advantage of any of the social activities available on campus?"

"Not likely. I haven't met anyone that I find particularly interesting, and the social events seem pretty high school to me. The few women I have attempted to get to know seem turned off when they learn I am a Vietnam vet. It puts a damper on things from then on."

"Jason, are you drinking more now?"

"More than what? Are you kidding? On the weekends, I am drinking myself to sleep every night. It's the only way I have to relax after spending all my time studying during the week. But that studying doesn't seem to help with my grades."

"Jason, I am going to share something with you that I hope you keep in confidence. I suffer from the same condition you are describing. It's called PTSD, or post-traumatic stress disorder. Those of us who have experienced extreme and often multiple combat suppressed our responses then and now suffer the consequences of that suppression. It is different in each veteran, but there are ways to manage them."

"Son of a bitch, Captain. You mean we all have the same problem?"

"No, not all of us. Mine didn't manifest until I was assigned as the notification officer for those killed in action in Vietnam. Those were emotional events that triggered mine."

"What the hell can I do? Right now, I am close to academic probation, and I don't see things improving next semester."

"Jason, you need to be clinically evaluated just as I was. If you permit me, I will contact Dr. Johnson at Louisville General Hospital and recommend she see you. What do you think?"

"I am all in, sir. Things can't be much worse. Here is my phone number. You can reach me whenever you want."

Jason Grundy left my office with a step that seemed more energetic than when he first entered. I now had a mission to support another Vietnam veteran. My call to Dr. Johnson was delayed until the next day, when she returned my call during my break between classes.

"Dr Johnson, Shirley, thanks for returning my call. I have a young Vietnam veteran who seems to be experiencing PTSD in much the same way I am. If you could see him, I think he could be helped in much the same way you have helped me."

"Captain Foster, I would be glad to see him. Please give him the number to call to schedule the appointment. I will be looking for him. What is his name?"

"It's Jason Grundy, and he will probably try to get up to Louisville on a three or four-day weekend we have in the Fall semester. Thank you again."

"How are you doing, Jim?"

"Taking it one day at a time, Doc. My boss is very supportive, and I am taking the steps both you and Jack Marshall suggested. They help."

"Good to hear, Jim. Let me know if I can help."

"Will do, Shirley."

I immediately called Jason Grundy and gave him Dr. Shirley Johnson's number to call for an appointment. He said he would call right away and tell me after class next week when he would be going to Louisville. With that favorable outcome, I thought it might warrant a date night with Alene. A call to her was met enthusiastically, and we thought the Boone Tavern in Berea would be a great place. As we drove leisurely to Berea, I told Alene about my experience with young Jason Grundy. Her response was a little surprising. I expected she would be glad to hear that I had been proactive in helping Grundy. Instead, she expressed concern that I shared my PTSD experience with a student. My explanation was that if I could help one Vietnam veteran with PTSD, I would share my experience multiple times over.

Her response made it clear to me that my explanation was not what she was looking for. It put a pall over our planned date night dinner. I couldn't understand why she thought it inappropriate to do what I did with another Vietnam veteran, particularly one who appeared to be suffering as I do from PTSD. Our small talk during dinner was at best perfunctory—the drive home in silence with Alene sitting straight and looking ahead the entire time. When we arrived home, Alene said she was going straight to bed, as she had a full day ahead of her the next day. No "goodnight" and no indication of what we had experienced in the evening. I retreated to the second bedroom that was now my home office. The favorite bottle of good Kentucky bourbon was right where I left it three weeks ago. Three good shots later, I was feeling no pain. Before I knew it, I had fallen asleep on the small couch in the office, only to be awakened by the slamming of the front door as Alene left for her volunteer work at the local Red Cross office. I recognized the shitty, hungover feeling that I hadn't felt for more than a month. I just couldn't understand what had turned off Alene. Did I do something wrong in my interactions with Jason Grundy? I didn't think so. I wonder if Jack or Shirley might help me understand what had happened.

The lack of an answer to either phone call did little to alleviate the sense of bewilderment I now felt. I left a message on Dr. Johnson's answering machine, but she probably wouldn't see it until later. A quick shower and shave did little to improve my attitude. As I left for the office, I was glad that I had no classes today. In my current state,

I would not be a good instructor. The more I thought about our conversation last night, the more the anger began to build. How can Alene judge me for trying to help another veteran suffering as I am? I know she doesn't understand, but dammit, she needs to trust me more than she does. I couldn't believe that our first significant disagreement was about my helping other veterans. It just didn't make sense.

Bob's knuckles rapping on my desk jolted me back into an awareness that I wasn't alone in the office.

"Hey, Jim. You look like you lost your best friend. What's up?"

"Alene and I had our first real fight since we were married. I am having a hard time figuring out what went wrong."

"Good luck with that. I am never sure what I did wrong until Barbara tells me. You might try asking."

"Believe it or not, Bob, she is upset that I am helping other Vietnam veterans who may be suffering from PTSD. I get the impression she thinks I shouldn't."

"I can't help you there, old buddy. There may be something more that is bothering her. Why don't you ask?"

My nonchalant response discouraged further discussion, and Bob soon left for his class. As I considered Bob's suggestion to ask Alene, I began to wonder if there were any support groups or systems available for veterans at the University. If there were, it might give some basis for my efforts and even convince Alene that I was doing the right thing. Over the past year, I have had the opportunity to get to know several university administrators, particularly those in the student support offices. If anyone would know about veteran services, it would be them. My first point of contact was a phone call to Ann Brandly in the Student Services department. It was no surprise when she told me that there are no student services for military veterans. Furthermore, she indicated that there were no current indications that such services were needed. I thanked her for the information and wondered how many veterans would be in school, and if that number was large enough, whether there should be some services to address their specific needs. I knew how hard it was for me to navigate the paperwork required to use my GI Bill. Student veterans must surely have this same challenge. I didn't know anyone in Admissions and Enrollment, so a phone call probably wouldn't give me the information I wanted. After a quick lunch, I walked to the Administration Building and knocked on the door of the Dean of Admissions.

A soft, "It's open," brought me into one of the older offices on campus. Behind a large, document-covered desk, a thin man in a maroon cardigan sweater looked at me behind large, clear-framed glasses.

"Ah, Captain Foster from the ROTC Department. How can I help you?"

"Dean Caldwell, I am a Vietnam veteran and was wondering how many other veterans may be attending Southern? My purpose in having that information is to provide services to those veterans when and if they need them. Without knowing how many there are, it's impossible to estimate how many services they may need."

"Captain Foster, that is an admirable effort. I assume you know that the admissions process doesn't include any information about an applicant's veteran status. Student accounts might know how many are using their veteran benefits, but otherwise, I am not sure we can assist. That said, many long-time staff here at Southern are veterans, including myself. I am confident that any effort you start would be welcomed by student veterans and supported by staff members."

"Dean, thank you. I was surprised that the school doesn't have any record of veteran admissions. I thought applicants supplied all the information."

"A fair assumption. However, I can contact the head of student accounts and obtain some of the information you are seeking. Give me your phone number on campus, and I will call you as soon as I learn how many students are using their veteran benefits."

"Thank you, Dean. I look forward to hearing from you."

The walk back across campus was a little brighter—another ally in the Dean of Admissions. Whatever we come up with, he is a supporter. I wonder how student services will respond when I have the numbers.

Chapter Thirteen: Student Veterans

It seemed like classes were improving. It might have been because I had a better attitude. Students were more engaged, and I left each class feeling energized, knowing that I had accomplished something important. That was until Jason Lundy came to my office late one day.

"Captain Foster, I just can't cut it. My grades are in the toilet, and I can't seem to get anything done. I am not scheduled to see Dr. Johnson until Spring Break, and I don't know that I can make it that far."

"Jason, have a seat and tell me where you are having the biggest problem."

"I still can't concentrate on my readings. As a history major, this is about all I do. Do you have any suggestions?"

"How many classes do you have this semester?'

"I'm only taking four. I need twelve hours to be a full-time student and be eligible for my GI Bill. The readings for your class are about the same as the others."

"Are the other three classes history courses?"

"No, just two. The other is almost as hard because it's a biology course that also requires a lot of reading."

"Who are the professors teaching the other two history courses? If I am familiar enough with them, I might be able to see what they can do to lighten your load, at least until after Spring Break."

That would be a big help, sir. Dr. Arnold teaches the World History class, and Dr. Richter teaches the American History class. Mrs. Wilson is the biology instructor.

"Jason, hang in there. I think the appointment with Dr. Johnson is important, and we don't want you to lose out on your academics before then."

"I'll try, sir. I have cut down on the booze. It wasn't easy, though."

"It's a start, Jason."

I had now made a promise I wasn't at all sure I could deliver. I knew Richter fairly well. He was one of my professors when I was a student, and he seemed to have been on campus forever. Arnold was an unknown. I knew he was new to the History Department, but that was about all I knew. Getting time to talk with each other wasn't much of a challenge. As a teaching member of the History Department, I was invited to the once-a-month social, usually held at the Department chair's home just off campus. The social was scheduled for this coming Friday, and I had already given the department secretary my RSVP to attend. I wasn't sure how Alene would feel about attending the social. I had only attended one before, and I don't recall many wives at that one. It was a pleasant surprise when Alene said she looked forward to the social and meeting some of the faculty I interacted with on campus. Maybe she wasn't still upset with me.

Alene and I arrived at the home of the Department Chair to find that most of the faculty were already there and enjoying some of Dr. Rutledge's wine. Paige Rutledge greeted us warmly and took Alene by the arm as she introduced us to the other couples. I recognized Dr. Richter immediately and was welcomed with a warm handshake and a smile. Before I had a chance to talk with him, Paige Rutledge introduced us to what she described as "the department bachelor," Dr. George Arnold. His greeting to Alene was warm, whereas his greeting to me was cold and perfunctory. As Alene turned to see someone she knew, Arnold's look at me was both questioning and dismissive. It was almost as though he considered me an outsider, someone to be overlooked in the social gathering. My initial thought was that asking Arnold for any consideration for Jason Grundy would probably be a lost cause. It also raised the question: What was the basis for Arnold's animosity? After a couple of minutes of small talk with the other faculty members, I approached Dr. Richter. Before I could say anything, he opened with.

"Jim, I am glad to see you on the faculty. I've heard good things about the military history class you're teaching. I would bet that your class will be full next semester."

"Thank you for the kind words. I am enjoying the opportunity and hope to continue teaching in the future. I have a student in my class that I want to discuss with you whenever you have some time."

"I am in my office on Mondays at least an hour before my first class at 10 and the second class at 2. Drop by anytime then."

"Thank you, Dr. Richter. I will see you on Monday."

The rest of the evening turned out to be surprisingly enjoyable. Alene recognized a few of the faculty wives from her work at the Red Cross and seemed to appreciate the chance to socialize with them. Only Dr. Arnold deliberately avoided me the entire night. I made a mental note to ask Dr. Richter on Monday why Arnold was so aloof. During the short drive home, Alene shared details about the wives she knew and gave me a rundown on the latest departmental gossip. She also mentioned a comment she received from another wife about Arnold. According to this other faculty wife, Arnold came to Southern after earning his doctorate from the University of California, Berkeley, and was an outspoken critic of the Vietnam War. Now I understand Arnold's cold attitude. He disliked anyone in uniform, whether civilian or military. To him, I was a "war machine," and he wanted nothing to do with me. I wonder if he knows Jason Grundy is a Vietnam veteran. If he does, I can't imagine how harshly he would treat the young man. The conversation with Dr. Richter has now taken on a whole new significance.

Saturday was as pleasant a fall day in Kentucky as we could have ever asked for. Alene fixed a picnic lunch, and we headed for the local regional park. I remembered the park as a place we came to party and drink beer when I was an undergrad. Now it seemed more of a family place for picnics and kid-focused parties. While we ate our picnic lunch, I told Alene stories about the Dr. Richter I knew as an undergraduate history major. I told her how you could always tell who was taking a course for the first time and who had been in Dr. Richter's courses before. His monotone delivery did not do justice to the quick witticisms and historical anecdotes that dotted his lectures. Those of us who had taken another course with Dr. Richter were busy taking notes and listening. The first-timers

were often seen dozing off.

The most intense moment in Dr. Richter's classes was when President Kennedy was assassinated. We knew at the start of class that he had been shot, but little else. Someone had a transistor radio, and we listened to the news reports from Dallas. When Walter Cronkite announced that President Kennedy was dead, Dr. Richter put his head down on his desk. The class of about eighteen students quietly picked up their books and slipped out of the room. We all felt it was necessary to give Dr. Richter some space and let him have that time alone. When I looked at Alene, a small tear rolled down her cheek as she said,

"Jim, that makes me cry. We all experienced that historic time in so many different ways. You have given me a picture of Dr. Richter and other historians that I would have never seen otherwise. Thank you."

"You can tell how much I respect Dr. Richter. I learned more about history—not just the subject itself— from him than from any other professor. I hope he can offer some recommendations on how to help one of my students. The one I referred to Dr. Johnson for a possible PTSD evaluation."

Alene's look at me was cold. "What do you mean by recommendations on how to assist?"

"Alene, this young veteran is struggling. I am certain his PTSD keeps him on edge, and the demands of being a history major, particularly the reading requirements, seem overwhelming. I know I need to help, but I don't see a way to get it."

"Why are you so committed to this one student, Jim? It's not like he is anyone special, is he?"

"Alene, only those of us who have been in combat and experienced the fear and adrenaline rushes that come from that can fully appreciate what it does to the mind. I thought I had mine under control until the NOKs and the SAOs triggered me. The stress Jason puts on himself to study, particularly the large reading requirements, is making it difficult for him to succeed. The literature that Dr. Johnson provided tells me that failure for those with PTSD makes committing suicide 75% more likely. Jason is on the edge of failure."

"Oh, Jim. I still don't understand what is going on. Suicide? Really? Just because you fail a class?"

"That is what I have learned, and I have lost too many soldiers not to do all I can to keep from losing one more."

Alene's demeanor had changed almost immediately. She was no longer the bright, engaged young wife enjoying a picnic with her husband. She was now someone who had an unwelcome burden to bear. I was that burden. The forty-minute drive home was another silent criticism of my efforts to make a difference for another Vietnam veteran. I wasn't sure how I could navigate the two conflicting sides. I remember what Stankey said: " If she can't or won't support you, I don't see much chance of success for you in managing your PTSD."

That night, Alene's reactions to my attempts to help Jason Grundy struck me harder than I expected. It felt like another blow to my self-confidence. How can I explain to Alene that my efforts to assist Jason are closely tied to my struggles? When I help another veteran, I am also helping myself. Dr. Johnson's encouragement and even Jack Marshall's support won't mean much if I can't communicate to the woman I love how crucial it is for me to help other veterans. Trying to separate my efforts to manage my PTSD from my desire to support another veteran dealing with PTSD doesn't make sense.

The next morning, Alene told me that she was going to visit her parents in Columbus. I asked,

"Does this have anything to do with our disagreement?"

Her less-than-emphatic response, "I just need to visit my parents for a couple of days," did little to improve my understanding of her reluctance to support my decisions. I did hope that some time with her parents, particularly her Dad, would help her appreciate what I needed to do. As she left me with a perfunctory goodbye kiss, I made one last effort.

"Alene, if you can overlook all my failings as a husband, please remember that I love you with all my heart. I would do nothing to damage our marriage. I hope you realize that."

Her eyes were sad. "I know you love me, Jim. I love you, too. I am just not sure that is enough."

Her words left me more puzzled than ever. As I drove to campus later that morning, I tried to make sense of what she meant. Those thoughts were left aside for the time being as I planned to meet with Dr. Richter in the hour before his first class at 10:00. The steps of University Hall hadn't changed in four years. Dr. Richter's office was just as I remembered it from my student days. My knock on the doorframe was greeted with a quiet,

"Good to see you, Jim. Come on in and have a seat."

After I sat down in one of the wooden chairs that had probably been in the building since it was built, Dr. Richter asked,

"What's on your mind, Jim? I believe your classes are going well. What else could it be?"

"It's one of your students, Dr. Richter. Before I talk about him, I need to tell you a little about what has happened to me. I have been diagnosed with PTSD, or Post Traumatic Stress Disorder. During the World Wars, it was referred to as shell shock and sometimes as battle fatigue. I have learned that it manifests differently in each individual, but it is repression of significant stress, in my case, from combat. I believe one of your students, another Vietnam veteran, is suffering from PTSD as a result of his combat experience, too."

"Jim, this is not something I was aware of, but I do remember some of my uncles and family friends acting strangely after they came back from the war. Are there any treatments or a cure for PTSD?"

"Unfortunately, only treatments and therapies. PTSD is a psychological injury and, similar to the loss of a limb, it is not curable, only managed. I am working hard on managing mine. Your student, on the other hand, is not. My concern is that if he fails any of his classes, his PTSD will intensify. I am told that those with severe PTSD are 75% more likely to commit suicide."

"Good Lord, I didn't know anything about this! Who is the student and how can I help?"

"Jason Grundy is in your American History course. He tells me he is not doing well and seems overwhelmed with the readings. He is a history major, and the three classes he is taking compound his anxiety."

"Jason is in the Wednesday class. He started well this semester but has struggled since. It's too late for him to drop the class. Let me see what is ahead for that class, and I might be able to give him some breathing room for the rest of the semester."

"Dr. Richter, that would be great if you would. He can't drop the class because he would lose his GI Bill benefits if he weren't a full-time student. If you don't mind, may I have Jason meet with you in the next day or two?"

"Certainly, Jim. He should know my office hours. I suggest he come as soon as possible."

I saw Jason after his class with me and told him to see Dr. Richter as soon as he could. Jason thanked me and said he would.

I was busy with mid-semester grading and a challenging new course the PMS asked me to design. Alene's absence was a significant distraction, and I had to concentrate more than usual to complete the grading and read for the new course. I was more than happy to find Alene's car in the driveway when I returned home on Wednesday. I thought she might be gone all week. I was even more surprised when I opened the door to have her wrap her arms around me and whisper in my ear,

"Jim, I am so sorry. The last two days have been an education for me. You deserve more from me. I love you."

I was both delighted to hear her words and curious about her education. "I am so glad you are home. I love you more each day. How was the visit with your parents?"

Dad and I share a close father-daughter bond. I told Dad what I learned about PTSD and how it is affecting you. Dad has, or had, friends with PTSD, and he gave me a clearer understanding of what I must do and how I can help. One of the key points he emphasized was that those with PTSD need to reach out to others and, when possible, offer support. Well, I am going to be your number-one supporter and will do everything I can to help you and provide the support you need to help others.

"I always knew I married the most beautiful woman in the world. I believe she has the greatest heart to match her beauty. Thank you, sweetheart, for the vote of confidence. Together we will make it happen."

"Jim, tell me about the student you are helping. Is there anything I can do?

"I think there are a couple of things to do, and you will be in one of those. Let me talk with Jason and gather more information about veterans enrolled here before we make any major plans. How do you feel about inviting Jason to our house for dinner one night?"

"I think that would be lovely. Just give me a date and I will do something special."

"Sweetheart, anything you fix will be special."

Chapter Fourteen: Working the System

The rest of the week flew by. I finished the grading for the mid-semester grades and was well on my way to wrapping up the reading for the new course. I asked Jason to stay after class on Thursday.

"Jason, my wife and I would like to have you come to dinner at our house this weekend. Which works best for you, Friday or Saturday?"

"Thanks, Captain Foster. Can we do Saturday?"

"Certainly. Let me write down our address. Let's say, 6:30 and very casual.'

"Yes, sir. Looking forward to it."

A quick call to Alene confirmed we were all set for Saturday. I asked if there was anything I could pick up at the store on my way home. As usual, she said she had it under control.

Jason arrived promptly at 6:30. Alene greeted him cordially, and I offered him iced tea that I had made earlier. My attempts to make him feel more comfortable were not very successful. Alene, as usual, carried the day.

"Jason, how old are you?"

The surprise on his face was unmistakable. "I'm twenty-two, Ma'am."

"While we may look somewhat older, Jim and I are only three and four years older than you. For that reason alone, I would appreciate it if you would reserve Ma'am for someone much older and use my given name, Alene."

"Yes, Ma'am, I mean Alene."

"Thanks, Jason. That's more like it. Now tell me about your family, where you grew up, and what you like to do."

Over the next ten minutes, Alene and I learned more about Jason than I had in the two months I had come to know him as a student and fellow Vietnam veteran. Here was a young man from a troubled home who joined the Army at eighteen to escape that environment, succeeded as a young private, and then was sent to Vietnam at nineteen. Although he didn't share his Vietnam experience with us, I could tell from past conversations that his combat experience as a rifleman was at least as traumatic as mine. We also learned that Jason was helping at least two other student Vietnam veterans with their challenges in school. Jason was certain one had PTSD. He wasn't so sure about the other, but knew he was struggling as a student.

"Jason, are there any formal or informal organizations on or off campus that other Vietnam veterans might join? I have learned that getting veterans together is a way to manage PTSD."

"No, sir. Nothing on campus. None of the student organizations appeals to us, and, quite honestly, some of them don't want us as members. The saddest part is that the local VFW and American

Legion seem to be made up of World War II and Korean War veterans who somehow look down on Vietnam veterans. They act like their war experience was greater or more important than ours."

"How about we start a Vietnam veterans student organization on campus? Do you think we would have enough members to make it worthwhile?

"Gee, I'm not sure. I think there are four or five Vietnam veterans. It would depend on what we would do in the organization and how it would be attractive to other Vietnam veterans."

"Let me work with my contact in Student Affairs and see what can be done. I will keep you up to speed on what I learn."

The rest of the evening was a delightful dinner with Jason. Alene was her "hostess with the mostess" all evening. At one point, she had Jason laughing hard when she told him about my purchase of the dress blue uniform and how she thought I was ripped off because the pants didn't match the jacket. She knew about "breaking starch" in fatigues and gently teased Jason about not having a girlfriend.

The evening ended on a happy note with Jason thanking Alene for the best dinner he had eaten in years. He looked at me, "Captain, thank you for this. I believe I can make it now."

When I closed the door, I looked at Alene to find a tear running down her cheek. "Sweetheart, what's wrong?

"Oh, Jim. How many more young men like Jason need someone to care? We have to do this more often."

I kissed the tear away, looked into those beautiful blue eyes, "We will, Alene. I promise this is just the start."

On Monday, I checked in with Deputy PMS, Lieutenant Colonel Duncan, to inquire about how I could establish a Vietnam veteran organization on campus. He was supportive, but recommended I start with the school's Student Affairs office for guidance. I thought it best to check with Ann Brandly first and assess the situation for student organizations. She said that there were more than thirty student organizations, and any student could start a new one. The basic requirements were to have at least a dozen members, craft a charter that outlines the organization's purpose, have a faculty sponsor, and elect leaders. That seemed simple enough. I passed that information on to Jason and volunteered to be the faculty sponsor. I didn't expect his first question, however.

"Should we make this organization open to all veterans, or just Vietnam veterans?"

"Honestly, I hadn't thought about that. Do you think we have other veteran students here at Southern?"

"Captain Foster, I don't know for sure, but if it is a veteran organization by definition, it's open to all veterans."

"You're right. Why don't you ask any other veterans on campus and see if they are interested in forming a Veterans Club, as a sponsored student organization?"

Bringing Home the Cost of War

I didn't realize how organized Jason was until he told me, two weeks after our discussion, that he already had fifteen veterans interested in forming the veterans club. His enthusiasm was evident and infectious, and that must have convinced the others to join him. I invited the veterans to use the conference room in the ROTC detachment for their organizational meeting. I sat in the back and watched as Jason and Eli Cummings were elected President and Vice President of the newly established Southern Kentucky University Veterans Club. The fifteen were unanimous in their agreement as to the purpose of the club – to encourage, support, and mentor veteran students at Southern. I told them I was proud to support their charter and suggested that they begin brainstorming ways to accomplish that worthwhile purpose. I had to leave the meeting to teach a class, but learned later that the veterans' meeting lasted another hour and a half. That evening, I called Jason and congratulated him on his election, suggesting that he and Eli begin the approval process with the Office of Student Affairs. He hadn't learned that once the club became an approved student organization, they could request financial support from Student Affairs to support their mission.

Over the next two weeks, I assisted Jason and Eli in assembling the necessary paperwork to obtain Student Affairs approval. I was pleasantly surprised to see that there were five Vietnam veterans in the group. The remaining ten veterans represented a diverse range, including those who served in Korea and Germany during their enlistments. It meant that the group would continue to grow as more veterans decided to use their GI Bill education benefits at Southern.

My interaction with both Jason and Eli provided much-needed encouragement to my efforts to manage my PTSD. I now felt I had a mission, one that could make a difference for other Vietnam veterans. The formation of the group, Jason's efforts in organizing it, and his socializing with other veterans seemed to improve his mental state. He even reported that his grades were improving. It wasn't as easy as we initially thought. George Arnold, the anti-war faculty member, was on the Student Affairs advisory board and vehemently opposed the formation of the Veterans Club, arguing that it gave credence to the "warmongers." Fortunately, he was outvoted by the other members of the board. Jason received the official confirmation of the Veterans Club organizational acceptance just before the end of the Spring Semester.

Sadly, a Vietnam veteran who had not joined the Veterans club committed suicide in his off-campus apartment just before the end of the semester. Jason confided in me later that this particular veteran was "really screwed up." Many of the other Vietnam veterans encouraged him to join them for informal beers and even dinners out. He never joined them. The Veterans Club attended the funeral in Louisville, Kentucky. It was also an opportunity for Jason to take the other four Vietnam veterans to Dr. Johnson's office and introduce them. Shirley told me in one of her later phone calls that the introduction of those veterans was her first evidence that recruiting other veterans to join an organization made the difference she expected. She told me to keep up the good work; it was making a difference.

I seemed to be on track to improve my physical conditioning. We in the ROTC detachment were fortunate to have handball courts located in the lowest level of the football stadium and immediately accessible to us almost whenever we wanted to play. After I had been playing for a couple of weeks, none other than George Arnold showed up at the handball courts. I was standing at the only available court and asked Arnold if he wanted to join me in a game. Unsurprised by his curt response,

"I guess if you are the only one available, let's play a couple of games."

It was unclear how long Arnold had been playing handball, but he was a decent player. Fortunately, I had been playing handball for many years and could hold my own. He started strong and just eked out a 21-19 win in the first game. I took the second game 21-15. The third game was a tough one. I could tell that I was out of shape, and fortunately so was he. The two of us lumbered around the court, almost exhausted, to a 20-20 stalemate. To win, one of us had to score two more points than the other. Both of us looked at each other and realized we had neither the energy nor the desire to try for those two points. I extended my hand to Arnold,

"Let's call it a draw, and we can finish our set some other time."

A thin smile was followed by, "You know, Foster, when the war comes to the streets of America, I will be on the other side."

"I know that, George. Just remember, my Army and I have a lot more experience at that than you and your Army."

I could see him mulling that thought over as he left. It turned out that George Arnold was a lot more bark than bite. Throughout the summer, we played six or seven times. Each time we were evenly matched, and I won just as many times as he did. Only once did he ask me about my experience in Vietnam.

"Jim, we hear so many conflicting stories about Vietnam. You spent some time there. What did you do?"

"I agree, there is so much in the news about Vietnam that I cannot relate to. Throughout my two years in Vietnam, we were up against the North Vietnamese regular army. They were well-equipped, well-trained, and tough. I can't speak to the geopolitical issues, but I do know those guys were trying to kick us out of South Vietnam, and our national leadership had decided we would support the South Vietnamese people and government. If we, as a people, believe that the decision is wrong, we need to address it with those who made the decision. We soldiers are given a mission. We accomplish that mission to the best of our abilities."

The look on his face demonstrated that he had not heard this particular take on Vietnam. He seemed to grasp the concept that it is useless to criticize the tool rather than its users. From then on, our relationship mellowed. I was able to explain to him that too many of the young men drafted for the conflict in Vietnam were ill-suited for their roles as combat soldiers. Their combat experiences damaged their already fragile psyche, and we, as a nation, were doing little or nothing to help them after they were discharged. I even tried to explain what PTSD was and how those suffering manage it. George is an intelligent academic, and I believe he did some research on his own, so I can't take all the credit for the changes in his outlook on the war. Handball may not have recruited another ally on campus, but it certainly changed an opponent into someone no longer opposing Vietnam veterans on campus.

Chapter Fifteen: Looking Back

During our last year in Leesburg, Alene and I grew to enjoy the campus and town more each month. She had taken a couple of the new veteran's wives under her wing and was helping them adjust. She thrived in her role as a "mother hen" to young wives. In one of our more intimate moments, she confided in me that she was considering returning to school to earn a master's degree in counseling. From that moment on, I knew that she had found her calling. She was soon accepted into the program at Southern and began working towards becoming a licensed guidance counselor.

For my part, the PTSD was still there. I recognized its effects on me and learned to manage them. During our last year at Southern, I was in the NOK and SAO rotation with all the other officers. I conducted two, one NOK and one SAO, as the war in Vietnam began its inevitable drawdown. They were tough, and I would be kidding myself if I didn't react as I had before. The difference was that I knew how to manage those reactions. Talking them over with Alene was the first step. Even sharing some of them with the Veterans Club made a big difference. I also found that "journaling," or writing down my feelings and responses, made a big difference. If I could put into words what I was feeling, I managed those responses in a way I couldn't before. While I didn't stop drinking altogether, I drank very little and only socially with others.

Bringing Home the Cost of War

When we prepared to leave Southern for our next assignment, it was a bittersweet experience. I will never forget those first NOK and SAO assignments. The memories of the families that received the message I carried will be with me forever. Their sense of loss reminds me daily that the cost of war falls as much on the families as it does on the soldiers in the fight. If nothing else, they strengthened my resolve to do everything possible to support the soldiers I led, wherever and however that was possible.

By contrast, there were moments, such as those with students in the classroom, the Veterans Club, and other ROTC events, that were highlights of the last year. When the Veterans Club learned Alene and I were leaving, they hosted a farewell dinner for Alene and me the week before we left. The current club President gave me far too much credit for establishing the club. Alene was presented with a framed picture of the club members with their wives and four of their children, which they had specially prepared for her. The heartfelt comments written on the margins brought tears to her eyes as she accepted the gift, indicating how much she appreciated their acknowledgement of her efforts.

As I work to bring this story to an end, I realize I have embarked on a journey of reflection—a memoir that finds its roots at my alma mater, Southern Kentucky University. It feels fitting to conclude this narrative with a glimpse into the remainder of my Army career. Alene and I dedicated another twenty-five fruitful years to the Army, culminating in my retirement as a Colonel from my last assignment at the Pentagon. During this time, I had the honor of commanding both an Infantry Battalion and an Infantry Brigade, experiences that defined my professional life.

During my service, I found myself on the staff of two Chairmen of the Joint Chiefs of Staff, navigating the complexities of military leadership and strategy. Thankfully, I never had to endure the harrowing responsibilities of a Next of Kin (NOK) notification or a Survivor Assistance Officer (SAO) duty again. Those three years of ROTC duty, intertwined with the emotional weight of NOK and SAO assignments, profoundly shaped my development as a leader, mentor, and father. Even now, remnants of my experiences cling to me in a very abbreviated form of PTSD, surfacing as sudden outbursts directed at "stupid drivers" or the occasional frustration at "idiots on television." Though they may sometimes feel like the rants of a senior citizen who has witnessed countless things and made a difference in the lives of thousands of soldiers, these moments are tinged with a deep-seated refusal to tolerate "bullshit" in any form.

Reflecting on my twenty-eight years of military service, I recognize numerous significant accomplishments, but none resonate with me more than my commitment to supporting veterans at Southern Kentucky University. What began as a humble veterans' club blossomed into a vital organization known as the Office of Military Support (OMS). This dedicated office passionately strives to assist veterans, active-duty soldiers, sailors, marines, airmen, and military families engaged with Southern, creating a nurturing environment amidst the academic community.

In the early 2000s, the OMS and its initiatives garnered national acclaim, earning the prestigious title of the nation's number one "Veteran Friendly" college or university. The founders of the Veterans Club, Jason Grundy and Eli Jackson, were celebrated as distinguished alumni during the 2015 Alumni Celebration. Their acceptance of this honor was particularly poignant, highlighting their pivotal roles in establishing the club and their impactful careers in education. Both Jason and Eli went on to expand their education, becoming inspiring high school history teachers and eventually high school principals.

As I read about their accolades and heartfelt testimonies in the online alumni newsletter, a deep sense of pride enveloped me, affirming that Alene and I had truly made a lasting difference in the lives of our fellow veterans and the broader community. More importantly to me, it was also how I learned to manage my PTSD.

PTSD: Why and What

Post-traumatic stress disorder (PTSD) is a mental health condition caused by a highly stressful or frightening event or events, either experiencing it firsthand or witnessing it. Symptoms can include flashbacks, nightmares, intense anxiety, and uncontrollable thoughts about the event. (Mayo Clinic). Although there are many treatments now available, few were available to many returning from Vietnam.